Welcome to Camp Creeps

HeebieJeebies
#2

Welcome to Camp Creeps

Rod Randall

Created by Paul Buchanan and Rod Randall

BROADMAN
&HOLMAN
PUBLISHERS
Nashville, Tennessee

© 1998
by Rod Randall
All rights reserved
Printed in the United States of America

0-8054-1195-X

Published by Broadman & Holman Publishers,
Nashville, Tennessee
Acquisitions Editor: Vicki Crumpton
Page Composition: SL Editorial Services

Dewey Decimal Classification: F
Subject Heading: FICTION—JUVENILE/FICTION—CHRISTIAN
LIFE/HORROR STORIES
Library of Congress Card Catalog Number: 98-14295

Library of Congress Cataloging-in-Publication Data
Randall, Rod, 1962–
     Welcome to Camp Creeps / Rod Randall.
             p.   cm. — (Heebie Jeebies series ; v. 2)
     Summary: While vacationing in the mountains, thirteen-
year-old Heather and her younger brother Todd call upon God
to help them when they stumble upon a deserted Christian
camp haunted by a dark phantom and a fierce beast.
     ISBN 0-8054-1195-X (pbk.)
     [1. Camps—Fiction. 2. Christian Life—Fiction. 3. Horror sto-
ries.]
     I. Title.   II. Series
PZ7.R15825We   1998
[Fic]—dc21

                                                     98-14295
                                                       CIP
                                                        AC

3 4 5 02 01

DEDICATION

For Taryn

CHAPTER 1

Pine needles snapped under my feet as I stumbled through the dark night. My little brother, Todd, had just swiped my flashlight and run ahead before I could get it back. That he got away from me wasn't just annoying, it was amazing. Normally he moves like a barge. With his thick ankles and pudgy frame, he's anything but fast.

"Wait!" I shouted, glancing from side to side. I had never been in these woods before and wasn't about to be stranded alone. Talk about creep central! The trees looked alive, like they were following me.

"Forget you, Heather the Feather," Todd yelled over his shoulder.

That did it! I was tired of Todd making fun of my weight. Or, more precisely, my lack of it. My *real* name is Heather Marie Pierce. I have reddish-blond hair, and twenty-three freckles on each cheek (if you want to get technical, it's actually twenty-six and twenty-eight, but in my opinion some are too small to count). Sure, I'm kind of skinny. But I'm thirteen and Todd's only eleven. I'm also taller than he is, which means I'm still his *big* sister.

I started to run as fast as I could, determined to catch the little pest. He would be sorry this time.

The wind howled through the branches above as I jumped rocks and ducked under branches. The twigs I couldn't dodge, I pushed out of the way. *Nothing to it,* I thought.

Wham! I plowed right into a tree and fell to the ground.

"Where did that come from?" I murmured.

Rubbing the lump on my forehead, sticky with sap, I sat there in a daze. Everything seemed blurry. Then an eerie sound caught my attention. Pine needles crunched nearby. Something was coming! Suddenly, two pale yellow lights came into focus. They inched through the shadows, closer.

I waved my hand and was greeted by a vicious growl. Whoever or *whatever* was behind those eyes was *not* in a good mood.

"Todd?" I yelled. No response. I strained my

eyes to look down the trail. More darkness.

The fiery eyes pushed forward, crunching the matted earth with each step. Two rows of razor-sharp, white teeth flashed in the night. The beast grumbled with hunger. *Grrrrr.*

Scrambling to my feet, I took off again. I sprinted as fast as I could. Dead branches scraped at my skin like claws, but I kept going. The trail widened. Glancing back, I couldn't see a thing. *Where was it? What was it?* I kept running, not wanting to find out.

"Todd!" I shouted, determined to track him down, "Get back here right now!"

The growls stopped. Was the beast running ahead to cut me off?

I could see my flashlight up ahead. Todd must have gotten scared and waited for me. Not that I blamed him.

Keep running, I told myself. *Ignore the sideache.* The flashlight was just ahead. But it wasn't moving. It was perfectly still. Another fifty feet and I'd be there.

I was breathing hard. Closing in. The flashlight still hadn't moved. What happened? How could Todd hold so still? And why wasn't he answering?

Twenty more feet. Almost there.

"Todd?" I screamed.

I stopped in horror. The light stood straight up in the center of the trail.

Todd was nowhere to be found.

CHAPTER 2

I picked up the flashlight and searched in all directions. "Todd," I demanded, "knock off the tricks and get over here. Now!"

No answer. Black silence. I could hear myself breathing. But nothing more.

I took a few more steps down the trail. I remembered the growling beast and yellow eyes. I feared the worst. "Todd?" I begged, my voice trembling.

A broken voice moaned back. "Over here."

I shined my flashlight in the direction of the sound. It was my brother, face down in the dirt. He turned toward the light. Blood dripped from his mouth.

"What happened to you?" I kneeled beside him, ready to cry. He could be a real pest sometimes, but I still loved him.

"It's too late," he whispered. He motioned me closer with trembling fingers. "Give Mom . . . ."

"What?" I asked, holding his hand.

He coughed and tried to speak.

"What?" I lifted his head.

"This—" He jumped up and planted a big, wet kiss on my cheek.

"Gross!" I hollered, wiping it off.

"Sucker," he taunted. He waved an open packet of ketchup in my face. "McDonald's is my kind of place."

"Now you've had it." I pinned him down and tickled his armpits. He laughed hysterically and begged me to stop. When he had suffered enough, I let him up.

Then I told him about the vicious growl and yellow eyes.

"Are you serious?" he asked, looking around. When he turned back to me, his scheming eyes betrayed him.

"What are you thinking?" I replied, as if I didn't know.

As soon as Dad had told us we would be spending the weekend in the mountains, Todd's imagination had taken over. For months he had been carrying around a book on trapping. He dreamed about catching wild animals and turning them into pets. "We'll start our own backyard zoo," he had announced. "People will pay us big bucks just to have a look." He went on to explain how his snares and cages would catch everything from raccoons to red-tailed hawks.

"This could be just the opportunity I was hoping for," Todd said.

"Yeah right," I scoffed. "We're not talking about a raccoon here. We're talking about a deadly beast that eats raccoons for lunch."

"Fear not, Sis," Todd assured me. "You've seen my book on trapping. I read part of the *entire* thing."

"You mean you looked at the pictures," I reminded him.

"Whatever. The point is I know what I'm doing," Todd explained. "Besides, if the so-called *beast* you saw really exists, kids will pay top dollar just to see it. We'll be rich."

"Yeah, right. More like dead. Let's get out of here."

Todd searched the night while biting his lip, then shrugged. "I think you're overdoing it a bit, but just to be safe, maybe we should find a different way home. First thing tomorrow, I'll come back and set a tree snare."

That sounded fine to me. But this time *I* held the flashlight and *I* stayed in front. As the older sibling,

I was used to being the leader, especially on family vacations. We walked a little farther and I tried to get my mind off of whatever it was that had growled at me. It helped to see the stars peeking through the branches above us.

Then a different kind of light caught our attention.

We spotted what looked like a street lamp shining through the trees, way up high. Soon several buildings came into view, surrounding the brilliant light. At least they used to be buildings. They were all dark. Some had been boarded up. Others had been burnt down.

Making our way to the lamppost, we realized that we were in the center of an abandoned camp. On both sides of us, the ground sloped uphill. To the right of the lamppost, several large buildings made of stone and wood dominated the hillside. To our left, a dozen or so small cabins clung to the earth.

We decided to check out the larger buildings first. The nearest building to the right had two stories and long, tinted windows that formed the front wall. The windows looked out over the rest of the camp. Wiping away the dust, we used my flashlight to peer inside. Broken tables and folding chairs littered the large room.

"Looks like we found the mess hall," Todd said.

"*Mess* is right," I replied.

We stepped back to survey the other buildings. One was long with an A-frame roof. Others further up the hill looked like dormitories. To the right of the mess hall, a drained Olympic-size swimming pool hid behind a chain-link fence.

"This is boring," Todd said. "Let's check out the cabins. Maybe one of the campers left something cool behind." He tromped down the hill to the lamppost, then slowed as he worked his way up to the cabins.

I followed along but stopped when I saw how bad they looked. The rickety dwellings were covered with moss that did its best to hold the boards together. In some cases the moss wasn't enough and the roofs had caved in anyway.

"What's wrong?" Todd asked.

I pointed at the cabin he was approaching. "Forget going in there. If a pinecone drops on the roof, the whole thing will collapse on your head."

"Come on, Heather the Feather," Todd teased. "Don't be a chicken."

I would have chased him down for that remark but didn't want to get any closer to the cabin. An engraved sign that read "Millview" dangled from a rusty nail.

"That should say *Mildew,*" I noted. "Look how green the wood is." By now I was ready to go. With its many abandoned and crumbling buildings, the camp reminded me of a ghost town from the Old West. When I told Todd, his eyes lit up and he didn't want to leave.

"How cool!" he announced. "A real live ghost camp. Awesome!" He moved to a grassy area between two cabins.

"You mean scary," I told him. "Let's get out of here."

"Stop being such a baby," he snapped back. Before I could stop him he disappeared behind one of the cabins.

Instantly, I heard a terrible scream.

"Heather!" he wailed. "Heather! Heather!"

"I'm not going to fall for that one again," I yelled back.

A moment later, he bolted into the clearing.

"I'm not that dumb," I told him. But as I shined the light on his face, I gasped.

He wasn't joking.

He looked scared to death.

CHAPTER 3

Todd's face was as white as a soldier's tombstone. "There's something back there! A ghost . . . or phantom."

"Get real. Ghosts don't exist. And you don't even know what a phantom is."

"I do now," Todd said, grabbing my arm. "And they're not pretty. Go see for yourself."

I stared at the mossy old cabins. Fallen shingles littered the ground. Spider webs hung from the doorways. The boarded up windows gave me the creeps. *If only it were daylight,* I thought. *Camps are never this scary. Why did we have to come here at night? Oh well, time to be the leader,* I decided.

With each step, I prayed for the Lord's protection. Unlike me, *he* could handle anything.

I held my flashlight in front of me. The beam

moved from side to side, piercing the darkness. Todd stayed behind me, his hand on my shoulder. We turned the corner, teeth clenched, ready.

"Ahhh!" I screamed, hoping to scare whatever it was away.

Todd joined in.

I waved the flashlight all around, but there was nothing there. Around back we didn't see a thing. Nothing.

"Some phantom," I said.

"Maybe it's hiding in one of the buildings," Todd suggested, nodding toward the nearest cabin.

"If it's that big and scary, why would it be hiding from us?" I asked.

"Beats me," Todd shrugged.

"It doesn't exist," I told him.

He gave me a look. He really wanted me to check for myself. As much as I wanted to walk away, I had to prove that the phantom didn't exist—for Todd's sake. Muttering under my breath, I decided to take a quick look in the cabin. Climbing onto the porch, I shined the light inside. A few steel bunks lined the walls, each with peeling white paint. Black droppings littered the floor. It looked like a regular rat roundup.

"I dare you to go in," Todd challenged.

"No thanks. I'm not that stupid," I told him.

I looked again. Nothing but filth. Then something landed on the top of my head. It had spiny legs, lots of them.

"Get it off me!" I screamed. "Now!"

I shoved the flashlight into Todd's hands.

He looked worried but tried to sound casual. "It's just a spider."

"How big?" I winced.

Todd cringed and gritted his teeth. "If it were raining, it'd make a good umbrella."

"Do something!" I screamed, trying to hold still.

He lifted the flashlight to take a swing.

"Are you crazy?" I threw my hands up for protection. "You'll smash its guts in my hair!"

I bent over and shook my head until the spider fell from my hair. It was so big I could actually hear it land. Think about it. Have you ever *heard* a spider hit the ground? I wanted to stomp it to death, but feared it would grab my foot and flip me back and forth like a puppet.

"What were you thinking?" I asked, grabbing back my flashlight.

"I was going to kill the spider," Todd said.

"Or me," I fumed, ready to leave. "There's nothing here but bugs and dust. Let's get out of here."

"Whatever you say," he said.

But as I started to leave, Todd stood still, like an ice sculpture.

"Now what's wrong?" I asked, rolling my eyes.

"Shine the light over there." He pointed between the cabins at the edge of camp. His finger trembled.

I turned around just in time. A black robe floated through the air like a ghost. It had a face like a skeleton and no lips to cover its teeth. At the sight of the flashlight beam, it disappeared behind a cabin.

"Did you see that?" I asked.

Todd just nodded. His mouth hung open, like he could swallow a grapefruit. "I'm starting to think the sooner we leave, the better."

I fixed my flashlight on the building where the phantom had gone. If it came back I would be ready.

Suddenly my flashlight flickered and went dead. I checked the switch. Nothing happened. No light. Nothing.

"Oh great," I grumbled.

"That's weird," Todd said. "Don't batteries go dead *slowly?*"

"I thought so," I told him.

I smacked the flashlight into my palm. Still out.

I grabbed Todd's arm while backing toward the lamppost in the center of the camp.

"Maybe it was just an old sheet," I suggested.

"But it was black," Todd replied.

I shrugged. "So it was dirty."

"That's not funny, Sis," he told me.

Todd was right. There was nothing funny about it.

Suddenly, hinges squeaked on the other side of the camp. The door to the mess hall began to move. The phantom stepped into view and let out a cruel laugh that echoed through the night. When a breeze kicked up, the rotten boards creaked so loudly it sounded like every building would come crashing down.

"How'd he get over there so fast?" Todd marveled.

The phantom stepped in our direction. His cape lifted behind him like a pirate's flag in the wind. He moved closer while staring us down. His skeleton face glowed. Closer.

I grabbed Todd and we began to run. Our legs churned across the rocky clearing. Our arms swung wildly at our sides. Passing the lamppost, we scrambled into the woods. We picked up speed going down the trail. I could hardly see but I didn't care. We were on a nonstop flight to our parents.

But we were not alone.

Beside the trail, the beast howled. Todd's trap idea was starting to make more sense. One for the beast and another for the phantom would suit me fine. I thought of Dad saying we would have rest and relaxation in the mountains. "Just a weekend away as a family," he had told us. At first that sounded boring. But it was sounding better all the time.

"Faster!" I yelled at Todd.

We jumped rocks and dodged branches. The beast thundered after us, growling.

Our vacation lodge came into view. The place was massive, and looked like it was made of life-size Lincoln Logs stacked one on top of the other.

"Harder! Don't let up," I urged between rasping breaths.

The howling faded behind us.

We burst through the front door.

"Mom!" I yelled.

"Dad!" Todd added.

No answer.

I darted into the kitchen and gasped.

Dad was doubled over the table. His eyes were shut.

"Dad!" I shouted, shaking his arm.

He didn't move.

CHAPTER 4

D ad?" I pleaded in his ear.

"Heather! What's wrong?" Mom came running in.

"There's something wrong with Dad." I shook him again, but he didn't respond. Drool dripped from his mouth. His wavy, brown hair pressed flat against the table.

"He's asleep. The medicine he took for his headache knocked him out." Mom grabbed a napkin to dab Dad's mouth. "Besides, your father always drools in his sleep."

"Gross," Todd said, inflating his cheeks like he would throw up.

"Heather!" Mom demanded. She twisted me around to look at the bump on my forehead. "What happened to you?"

I was about to answer when my dad stirred from his sleep. He slowly opened his eyes and sat up. "What's all the yelling about?" he asked.

"Ask them," Mom said, sitting down. She pulled back her blonde hair and rested her chin on her knuckles, waiting for an explanation.

My dad slipped on his wire rim glasses, equally interested.

"You won't believe it," I started.

"We saw a phantom—" Todd added.

"And a werewolf," I continued.

Todd glared at me. "You said it was a beast."

"What do you think a werewolf *is*, a pet?"

Dad lifted his hands. "Slow down, slow down."

Mom offered a doubtful glance. "What are you two talking about?"

"We found a deserted camp," I gasped, pausing to catch my breath. "It was just like a ghost town."

"Haunted and everything," Todd put in. His eyes swelled up, like he was seeing it all again.

I described what had happened to us.

"Heather's flashlight even went dead," Todd said. He motioned for me to show them.

I slid the switch to "on." Nothing happened.

"Are you finished?" Dad asked, crossing his arms.

I knew what was coming.

So did my brother. "You don't believe us," Todd said, getting upset.

Dad shook his head. "I didn't say that. If you say you saw a deserted camp, I believe you. But as for a phantom or werewolf, I don't know *what* to say. It's obvious that something or someone scared you."

"Not me," Todd stated. "But you should have seen Heather. She was ready to cry."

"That's it," I said, grabbing Todd in a headlock. "Now you've had it."

"Hold on," Dad said. He pulled us apart. "Regardless of who was or wasn't scared, I don't want you to go back to that camp, at least not until I have a chance to check it out."

"That's for sure," Mom added.

Dad continued, "As for the phantom or beast, I wouldn't make too much of it. It's probably just someone with a sick sense of humor trying to scare you away."

Just then a creepy howl echoed through the room.

I raised an eyebrow. "You were saying, Dad?"

Mom grabbed Dad's arm. "I didn't know there were wolves in these mountains."

"Me neither," Dad said. He got up to look out the window. He pushed open the glass and stuck his head outside.

Suddenly Dad let out a howl, louder and louder. He sounded like a dog with its tail on fire.

Mom laughed and rolled her eyes. "Dear, what are you doing?"

Dad clenched his teeth. "Telling the wolf to get lost."

Todd and I laughed too. Then a different kind of growl filled the room. Like the one we first heard.

Dad started to scream!

We watched in horror.

"It's got me," Dad cried, leaning out of the window. His legs shook. His feet left the floor.

Mom ran over to help. But it was too late.

CHAPTER 5

Mom reached the kitchen window and cried out. "Dwight!"

"Dad!" we screamed.

She turned to us, then back outside. "Dwight! Dwight!"

Just then, Dad popped up out of nowhere. He grabbed Mom and gave her a kiss.

"Honey?" she asked, totally frustrated. "*What* are you doing out there?"

"Teaching this werewolf to *sit*," Dad answered with a grin.

Mom helped him climb back through the window. "Don't you think these kids have had enough thrills for one night?"

"You're right," Dad admitted. "I was only joking." He looked over at us. "Are you two really bothered by what you saw?"

We nodded.

"That's too bad," he said, putting his hands on our shoulders. "I really wanted this vacation to be a retreat for us. I, for one, need it. I was hoping for lots of fun times together, not worrying about some imaginary phantom at an old camp."

I grabbed his hand, almost pleading. "Dad, it's not imaginary. It's real. And I want to find out more about it."

Mom shook her head. "Your dad has already told you not to go back there. And I agree. It's too dangerous."

Maybe so, I thought. *But there has to be a way.* I tried a different approach. "We don't have to go to the camp to learn more about it. We can ask in town."

Todd returned from the microwave with a bag of popcorn. "Yeah! We can be investigators like you, Dad."

My dad works for an insurance company. He investigates claims when property is stolen or houses burn down. He's the best. One time he solved a case where the owner started a fire in his own house just to get the insurance money.

I watched Todd stuff a handful of popcorn into his mouth. After grabbing some kernels of my own,

I continued. "Please, Dad. It's just that I have so many questions."

Mom offered Dad a worried look. "Such as?"

"What happened to the camp?" I said. "And why does someone want to scare us away?"

Dad shrugged. "It's hard to say. God knows, of course. But perhaps we never will."

"But maybe we can help solve some kind of mystery." I gobbled a big handful of popcorn and reached for another.

"I doubt it," Mom said. She got up and poured us all some punch.

If only I had another comeback. But I didn't. For some reason I was feeling light-headed. I thought of the spider that had landed on my hair. Did it bite me before I shook it loose?

I couldn't breathe. I started to choke.

Everything looked blurry.

"The spider," I gasped. "Help."

"What is it, Heather?" Dad asked.

My head was spinning. "Air, please," I begged.

My lungs felt like they were caving in.

"She's passing out!" Mom shrieked.

Dad squeezed my hand.

By then I was gone.

CHAPTER 6

"H eather?" My dad pleaded, patting my back. "Heather, what's wrong?"

"Do something, Dad!" Todd begged.

"Hurry!" Mom cried out.

That was enough for me.

"Fooled you!" I said, laughing. I opened my eyes.

Mom crossed her arms and frowned.

Dad winked. "Fine. Now we're even."

I spun around and bowed low. "Thank you. Thank you very much."

"Great, a star is born," Dad said sarcastically. He stood up and rubbed his eyes. "Well, that's enough excitement for one night. It's time for bed."

The thought of getting sleep after a long day started a chain reaction. Pretty soon we were all yawning and stretching.

While Mom helped us unpack our pajamas, Dad locked up, which took a while because the lodge was so big. Talk about a house made for the mountains. Everything was wood—the floor, ceiling, walls, everything. The rooms smelled like a lumber yard.

A moose head with huge antlers hung above the fireplace. Whenever you walked into the den, its eyes always seemed to be staring right at you.

"Imagine trapping something *that* big," Todd said when he first saw it.

Our beds were in the loft. The railing was made of dry logs, polished smooth. Todd and I could have had our own rooms, but the loft was too neat to pass up. It had a door just like a normal room, but one wall was open to the den below. We could look down on the fire and listen to the logs crackle. The loft also had a huge window with a great view of the rocks and trees.

Before we went to bed, we knelt to pray as a family. Mom opened, followed by me, then Todd. Dad prayed last. "Dear Lord, we praise you for bringing Heather and Todd home safely. We're grateful for your love and protection. In Jesus' name, amen."

That made me feel better. As much as I wanted to find out about the camp, just thinking about it gave me the heebie-jeebies. When I climbed in bed, I pulled the covers up to my eyes.

I tried to sleep but couldn't, especially when Mom and Dad turned off all the lights downstairs. The tree shadows flickered on the window above my head when the wind blew. Todd was snoring next to me. When he first got in bed, he studied his book on how to trap wild animals. But he didn't last long.

Must be nice, I thought. *If only I could doze off too.* I tried quoting Bible verses and praying. That always worked before. But I still couldn't sleep.

Then something strange happened. Footsteps creaked across the wood floor downstairs. I could hear a muffled voice. But only one voice. Was it Dad's?

I lifted my head from the pillow. What was he saying? And to whom? I got up and moved quickly. But I could hardly see.

Ouch! My toes slammed into the door.

I grumbled under my breath.

The voice downstairs stopped. I froze, hoping I hadn't been heard. The voice started again. I quietly opened the door and crept to the stairs. The sound came from the hall closet. This time I moved carefully through the blackness, feeling my way along the railing. My feet slowly came down on each step. *Easy. Quiet.*

Then something grabbed me! Like a claw! It had my ankle and held tight. I tried to jerk loose but couldn't. It wouldn't let go.

CHAPTER 7

Let go! Let go!" I screamed.

"Shhh!" Dad ordered, standing beneath the stairs. After letting go of my ankle, he turned on the light. "What are you doing up?"

"I heard a voice," I explained, still trying to catch my breath. "I wondered what was going on." My heart was pounding so hard I could barely talk. My eyes searched the den, half-expecting the phantom to appear.

"That was me on the phone," Dad said. He looked bothered. "You should be asleep, not wandering around."

"But I couldn't sleep," I explained. "Besides, who were you talking to?"

He crossed his arms, "Sorry, Heather. That's none of your business."

"Why can't you tell me?" I asked. It seemed important.

Dad turned away like he had something to hide.

What's wrong? I wondered. *Is he in trouble? Why did he make the call in the hall closet?*

Dad started to say something, then stopped. He turned me around and marched me back upstairs. "Everything's going to be fine, Heather, as long as you stay in bed."

I wouldn't give up. "But what about—"

"Good night," he ordered, like he was warning me. "And don't get up again."

"But Dad—"

"Shhh." He placed his finger over his lips and went back downstairs.

First the camp, now the mystery with my dad, some vacation this was turning out to be. I pulled the covers *over* my head this time. I didn't want to look out the window at the black trees and sky. I had seen enough thrills for one night.

"Help me to fall asleep, Lord," I prayed. "The sooner the better."

It didn't happen right away, but finally I nodded off. God is good. He keeps watch over me no matter what.

I woke to the smell of bacon and coffee. Todd was gone. His bed was already made. *I must have overslept,* I thought. Jumping out of bed, I headed for the door. But on the way I felt a taunt string pull against my ankle. Before I could stop, it snapped loose. From the corner of my eye I spotted a thick object swinging for me, like a wrecking ball.

"Ahhh!" I screamed. I tried to duck but didn't make it in time.

Whomp! The object smacked me upside the head. I steadied myself, not sure I wanted to open my eyes.

"Yes! It worked! It worked!" Todd chanted, jumping into the room. "Todd the Trapper at your service!"

A pillow hung from the ceiling by a string. Todd had somehow rigged it to swing down as soon as I crossed the trip wire. I shook my head in awe. On the one hand it was a pretty ingenious trap. On the other hand, he was asking for it. With a quick jerk, I pulled the pillow from the ceiling and started swinging. "Trap this," I said, bringing the pillow down on his blond head.

"En garde," Todd replied. He used his arms as a shield. Before I could connect again he dove for my bed and took hold of my pillow. For the next few minutes we exchanged blows, swinging, ducking, and laughing until Mom called us for breakfast. I

gave Todd one last whomp for good measure and bolted downstairs.

By the time we reached the table, we were both so hungry we chowed down our pancakes and bacon in record time. Mom and Dad ate leisurely. They planned the day and sipped their coffee while listening to us brag about who won the pillow fight. After the spooky events of last night, they looked relieved to see us so happy.

Once we finished breakfast, Todd and I headed outside to explore the area around the lodge. A big boulder gave me a chance to show off my climbing skills. I zipped right to the top like I was climbing stairs. Being light can be a real blessing at times.

Todd didn't do so well. His boots kept slipping and his fingers got tired. Finally I helped him to the top. We stood on the peak like two brave adventurers. With Mom and Dad far below us, we felt like we had just conquered Mount Everest.

"Enough of this climbing stuff," Todd said. "I'm ready to set a snare for that werewolf. Do you want to come?"

I didn't. But because he had come climbing with me, I figured it was my turn to accompany him. After picking up some rope, a hammer, and a few other items that Todd had brought from home, we headed down the trail to where we had last heard the beast.

"This looks good," Todd said. He positioned himself beneath a long, green branch. After pounding a stake deep into the ground and grabbing the rope, he climbed the tree and shinnied out onto the branch.

I did my best to keep an eye on Todd while watching the woods for fear the beast would return. At least if I saw it coming, I could join Todd in the tree before it got to me.

"Almost there," Todd grunted, working his way along the limb.

"Careful," I warned him. "That branch might break."

"Bend, yes. Break, no," Todd replied. As he moved along, the branch continued to dip lower and lower like a catapult being set. Once he reached the end, Todd hung by his hands. The branch bent so low that his boots were within reach.

"Now what?" I asked.

"Pull me down," Todd said.

"You're crazy."

"Quick! I mean it."

Grabbing his ankles, I cringed, expecting the branch to snap and come crashing down on my head. But it didn't. I had to use all my weight but eventually got Todd to the ground. With one hand holding the branch and the other holding the rope, Todd quickly tied the branch to the stake. Then he motioned for me to stand back while he positioned a loop next to the stake.

"You really think that this will catch the were-wolf?" I asked him.

"Positive. When he steps in this loop and jerks the rope, the knot holding the branch to the stake will come free. The branch will fling through the air, taking whatever is in this loop with it."

"But why would anything *be* in that loop?" I asked.

"Here's why," Todd announced. He reached into his pocket and removed two pieces of bacon. He crumbled them up and placed them in the center of the loop. Then he tied a bell to the end of the branch. "When you hear the bell, it can only mean one thing: We've bagged the beast."

"Sounds good to me," I said, picturing those yellow eyes from last night. "The sooner the better." With that we headed back to the lodge to check in with Mom and Dad.

CHAPTER 8

We found Mom on the deck reading a magazine. "Where's your father?" she asked as soon as she saw us.

"We figured he was with you," I said with a shrug.

My mom removed a tissue from her pocket and dabbed her nose. She did that whenever she was nervous but didn't want us to know it. "Oh well. I'm sure he's around here somewhere."

"This sounds like a job for Todd the Trapper," my brother said, puffing out his chest. "Just give me a minute and I'll find him."

"Yeah right," I moaned, rolling my eyes. "You don't even know where to look."

Before Todd could offer a comeback, the bright ringing of a bell caught our attention.

Todd dropped his chest and his mouth fell with it. "The werewolf?" he gasped.

"Sounds like it," I said. "Come on, Mom." We jumped from the deck and headed into the woods. Pushing aside branches, we jogged toward the snare. The bell continued to clang like it was tied to a tiger's tail.

"Jackpot!" Todd said, running in front of me.

I peered through the trees, curious to see our catch. I feared what would happen if the animal got loose and came after us. What would we do? Run? Fight back?

Try *neither.*

When at last we arrived at the trap, we were too shocked to do anything.

Dad hopped beneath the branch with one foot on the ground and the other caught in the snare. He looked like one of those football players after punting the ball, only Dad's foot wasn't coming down.

"Is it true, Dad?" I asked, trying to keep a straight face. "Are *you* the werewolf?"

"No, but I may act like one if you kids don't get me out of this mess," Dad shot back. He explained that he had been out walking and didn't notice the rope. "I think you camouflaged the trap a little *too* well, Todd."

"Admit it, Dad," Todd replied. "You just wanted that bacon."

We ran over and helped with the knot, determined to free Dad as soon as possible.

But before we could, Mom arrived. She didn't seem rushed at all. "Now that's impressive," she said with a laugh.

"What is?" I asked. "Todd's ability to set a snare?"

"Actually, I was thinking of your dad's ability to do the splits," Mom chided. "Although, Todd's trapping technique isn't bad either."

We all joked back and forth while helping Dad get out of the noose. He still couldn't believe he hadn't seen the rope.

"My mind must have been someplace else," he suggested.

I thought of his secret phone call last night and wondered if that had anything to do with it. But I didn't ask.

Before we returned to the lodge, Todd wanted to reset the trap. With all four of us on hand to pull down the branch, it didn't take long before the snare was ready to go again.

After lunch, Mom agreed to take Todd and me to Mountain Creek. It was ten miles away, but still the nearest town. I wanted to find out as much as I could about the ghost camp, and Todd wanted to get some more supplies for his traps. Dad stayed behind to read and maybe soak in the hot tub.

The drive was long and slow because of the narrow, winding road.

"We're really in the middle of nowhere," I said. "It was dark when we arrived last night. I didn't realize how isolated the lodge was."

Our minivan rounded one sharp curve after another. When Todd's face turned green, Mom pulled over and we got out for some fresh air. The view across the gorge was beautiful, but I wanted to get going right away. I couldn't wait to find out more about the ghost camp. Besides, I needed to get batteries for my flashlight.

As soon as Todd's face returned to a normal shade of pink we finished the drive to town. Mom headed to the market to buy food, and we set out to play detective.

"Let's try there first," I said, pointing to Mountain Creek Hardware, a little store with stone walls.

"That place gives me the chills," Todd said. "But considering what we need, I guess it's our best bet."

The sign out front was falling down, and the windows were so dark they looked more like coal than glass, like they hadn't been cleaned for years. The door creaked when I pulled it open. My heart raced as soon as I stepped inside. *Why was everything so scary on this trip?* I wondered.

The store was cluttered with the kind of tools you would want in the mountains. Axes, saws, picks, that sort of thing. A thick layer of dust covered everything.

The clerk who worked there didn't seem very friendly. He had bony fingers and a scruffy, gray beard that grew in patches. He smelled like gasoline.

"Where are the batteries?" I asked him, hoping that when I bought something he'd be willing to answer some questions about the camp.

He tipped his head. "Down that aisle." His eyes stayed on me the whole way like he didn't trust me.

I located the batteries between the gloves and light bulbs, but I had to kneel down to find the right size. Then something strange occurred to me. I hadn't seen Todd since we came in the store. I stood up and searched around.

"Todd?" I said, raising my voice.

No answer.

"Todd?" I repeated, checking the other aisles. When I still couldn't find him I went to the front counter. The man who worked there was gone!

"Todd, where are you?" I demanded, pacing back and forth.

Then I heard his voice. He called out for me to help him.

"Heather!" he shouted. "Hurry!"

I ran toward his voice, to the back of the store by the cutting tools. I could hear him struggling. When I found him I knew why. He was on the floor with an ax dangling over his head. It was slipping off the rack.

"Todd, look out!" I screamed.

He lifted his eyes in horror as the ax fell.

CHAPTER 9

Todd rolled to the side just as the ax landed with a thud, cutting a gash in the floor.

I raced down the aisle, breathless. "Todd, are you all right? What happened?"

Todd sat there in shock. He looked at the thick blade, shiny and razor sharp.

"What happened?" I wanted to know.

"I tripped over a gas can. Then I bumped the wall." He looked up with eyes the size of golfballs. "That ax would've split my head like a block of wood."

"Well," I admitted with a grin. "You *do* have a blockhead."

"Funny," Todd said, getting to his feet.

The clerk with the patchy beard returned from the back room. "Is everything all right?" he asked.

Todd explained what had happened.

"You're lucky you weren't killed," the clerk muttered.

Todd nodded. "I think you should put the axes in a safer spot."

"I could," he grumbled. "Or you could watch where you're going. This ain't no toy store." Apparently he wasn't in the mood for some friendly advice.

I carried the batteries to the counter. Time to ask about the ghost camp, I decided.

But before I could, a ray of light sliced through the room. The front door creaked open. An old woman with red fingernails and yellow teeth stepped inside.

She gave us a weird look, then started to browse up and down the aisles.

Now's my chance, I thought. "I was wondering," I began, getting the clerk's attention. "Do you know if there used to be a camp in this area?"

He rung up the batteries, then glared at me. "What kind of camp?"

"A summer camp for kids," I explained. "With a mess hall, swimming pool, lots of cabins. That sort of thing."

He watched the woman walk to the far end of the store. Then he shook his head. "There could have been. But I haven't lived here long. I'm not much of an expert on these parts."

"No one has ever mentioned it?" I continued.

He put his elbows on the counter and spoke through clenched teeth. "Like I said, I haven't been here that long."

I grabbed the batteries and my change. "Thanks anyway."

Todd purchased a roll of chicken wire for his trap and we headed outside. The bright sun made me squint. "Why does the clerk keep that store so dark?" I wondered out loud.

"And dusty," Todd added.

"By the way, Todd," I said, remembering how frustrated I was with my brother. "Why didn't you answer me in there?"

"I did," he said, getting defensive.

"Not at first," I told him.

Todd just gave me a shrug.

"Let's get away from here," I said. "That store is almost as bad as the haunted camp."

We went to the market across the street, but the girl at the register was too busy to talk. We decided to try the post office. As we proceeded down the block, a shrill voice called from behind.

"Just a minute, you two." It was the old woman we had seen in the hardware store.

"Yes?" I answered, turning around.

She limped toward us and lifted a trembling hand. Wrinkles covered her skin. One red fingernail pointed in my face. "Did you say something about a summer camp?"

"Yeah. Do you know about it?" I asked, not sure what to think.

She clutched her purse and came closer. "Perhaps I do. What does it look like?"

"A total disaster," I admitted, stepping back. "The cabins are falling apart. Some are even burned down."

A grave expression came over her face, like she had remembered something awful that she didn't want to think about. "That's the one."

I sighed with relief. "Finally, someone who can help us."

"Don't be so sure," she cautioned. She put her hand on the back of my neck. Her eyes were hard. Her chin began to shake. She looked around to make sure no one was listening. In a quivering voice she told us, "There's something I think you should know."

CHAPTER 10

T odd gave me a worried look. He wasn't sure he wanted to hear this. I wasn't either, but it was too late.

"What?" I asked.

"That camp has a history. For years, it was a wonderful place for kids. They could swim, hike, ride horses. And best of all, they learned about the Lord."

"It was a Christian camp?" I asked.

She smiled. "Heavens, yes. Every week kids would hear the gospel and give their lives to Christ."

"What happened?" Todd asked.

The woman just stared at us, like she had said too much already. Her eyes began to water.

What is she afraid of? I wanted to ask. *Is the camp really haunted?*

The old woman looked up and down the street, then continued. "It's a sad story that I'd rather not get into. But I *will* tell you how it ended. A camper was attacked by a wild animal."

"What kind?" Todd immediately asked.

"A wolf," she replied.

I swallowed hard. I thought of those yellow eyes, the growls, the heavy footsteps that chased me through the woods. OK, so it wasn't a *werewolf*, but it was a wolf.

The old woman went on. "One night after a campfire, a boy decided to go for a night hike. He strayed from the trail and ended up out by the camp's boundaries. That's when the wolf started after him."

I'd heard enough for one day.

Too bad Todd hadn't. "What happened to the boy?" he asked.

The old woman shifted her attention to Todd. "The boy was about your age, you know."

Todd rolled his eyes. "Oh great."

The old woman kept talking. "That poor child came within a foot of his life. Good thing he climbed that tree. Lord knows what would have happened to him. When the counselors arrived, they ran the wolf off. But the boy was so shook up he had to go home."

"Did they ever catch the wolf?" I asked.

The old woman shook her head. "They never could find it. And believe me, they tried. Pretty soon registrations fell off. Parents were just too afraid to send their kids up here. Not with a wolf on the loose and all."

Todd scrunched his eyebrows together, discouraged.

"There were other problems too. Mysterious ones. The power would go out. Doors would fall off their hinges. Campers heard strange laughter in the night. No one wanted to come back. They finally had to close the camp." The old woman dropped her head in sorrow.

"That's too bad," Todd said.

She agreed. "After they abandoned the camp, some of the cabins were set on fire. But thank God the chapel's still in one piece."

"Is that the long building with the A-frame roof?" I asked.

The old woman nodded. "You should see it on the inside. It's absolutely beautiful."

The more I learned about the camp's fate, the worse I felt. I wondered how many kids had gone there to swim, hike, and learn about God. It must have been sad for them when they could no longer go. As unrealistic as it seemed, I wished there were something we could do to help. The old woman must have read my mind.

"I wouldn't go near that camp if I were you," she warned. "Something's not right about that place."

"No kidding." I said. "When we were there last night, we saw a phantom."

"Really?" She gave me a strange look, like she didn't believe me. Or maybe she did and felt suddenly afraid. Leaving us there, she limped down the street. "Take my advice," she warned. "Stay away."

As soon as we found Mom we shared the story with her. Then we told Dad back at the lodge. Our parents sided with the old woman.

"It's like we said last night," Dad stated, "You have no business being around that camp."

"But we *can't* just forget about it," I argued. "Let's go as a family. We'll be safe. And we can check out the chapel."

My dad wouldn't hear of it. "That's not possible."

I reached for my Bible. "But Dad. With God all things are possible. Isn't that in here somewhere?"

My dad raised his eyebrows and tipped his head. I was right, and he knew it. But soon a worried look came over his face.

What did Dad know that I didn't? I decided to ask. "Dad—"

Beep. Beep. Beep. It was Dad's pager. So much for asking him a question. He left to call the number flashing on the readout. After hanging up, he talked to Mom in private. A few minutes later Mom returned and quickly changed the subject

"Don't you think it's time you two checked the tree snare?"

When Todd agreed, I reluctantly followed him outside.

"What was that all about?" I asked Todd. "Since when is Mom so into animal traps?"

"Since she learned how cool they are," Todd replied, walking tall.

We found the tree snare empty and in the same condition as when we left it. But Todd wasn't discouraged.

"You know what they say," he offered. "Two traps are better than one."

We returned to the lodge so that he could get started on another trap with the chicken wire. After putting on leather gloves and grabbing some wire snips, he formed the wire mesh into a cage. Then he made a door for one end. The door would swing shut and latch tight simply by pulling a string. For bait, he dropped a handful of peanuts in the center of the cage.

"The key is to lure the animal into the trap, then close the door behind it," Todd explained. Backing away from the cage, he unwound the string over to the deck. "Now you just need to wait for the next hungry squirrel to come along. When it goes for the peanuts, pull the string."

"Excuse me? You really think a squirrel will walk inside that cage?"

"Yep. Good bait will bring them in every time."

"What do you mean, *every time?* You've never even tried this before."

"It's all in the book, Heather. Trust me."

"Yeah right," I laughed. "And why do *I* have to pull the string?"

"Because I need to set one last trap. I invented it myself."

"Oh brother," I sighed, taking the string from him as he walked away. "This I gotta see."

CHAPTER 11

With a shovel in his hand, Todd moved to a spot about fifty feet from the lodge. From my vantage point on the deck, I could keep an eye on him and the chicken wire trap at the same time. Todd dug a hole then pounded a stake into the bottom of it. Next, he tied a snare to the stake. When that was done, he covered the hole with pine needles and twigs.

"Let me guess," I offered with a broad grin. "An unsuspecting animal, like a grizzly bear for instance, steps in the hole and gets snagged by the snare. As he struggles to get away, you stroll up and wrestle him to the ground with one hand tied behind your back."

"Go ahead. Have your fun," Todd said. "But when the neighborhood kids are paying top dollar to see my wild animals, you'll be singing a different tune."

"I'll believe it when I see it."

"Oh ye of little faith," Todd chided.

"What do you mean? I've got tons of faith in God. It's your traps I'm not so sure about."

"Oh really? Well maybe you should have another look." Todd nodded at the trap made of chicken wire. A squirrel sat well inside the cage on its hind feet, cherishing a peanut in its little hands. "You were saying?"

"Beginner's luck," I replied, swallowing my pride. "But what can I say, it works." With a quick tug on the string, the door slammed shut behind the squirrel.

I braced myself, thinking the squirrel would bang and claw at the chicken wire, wild for freedom. But it didn't even notice that the door had slammed shut. It was too busy eating the peanuts— at least until we walked over to the cage. Then the fur ball went into overdrive, bouncing from side to side like it was in a pinball machine.

"Quick, let it out!" I yelled.

"But what about the zoo?"

"Do you want a *dead* zoo? It's gonna break its neck."

Grumbling to himself, Todd reached down and opened the door. The squirrel bolted for freedom and scrambled up the first tree in its path.

"Oh well," I said. "The main thing is, your cage trap works. Congratulations."

"What can I say?" Todd said, puffing out his chest. "I'm a natural."

After dinner I wanted to go for a hike and asked Todd to go along. He agreed, thinking maybe we could spook some animals into his traps. Mom and Dad stayed back to sip cappuccino on the deck and watch the sun set.

First we checked the tree snare, which was empty. Then we headed in the opposite direction of last night. I wanted to go toward the camp, of course—and so did Todd—but we couldn't. According to Mom and Dad, it was off limits.

Our hike started out fine. But it's easy to get lost in the mountains, especially when you're seeing things for the first time.

"Where are we?" Todd finally asked.

"Beats me," I said. The tree shadows seemed ready to smother us if we wandered off the trail. The sky grew darker by the minute.

"Here." Todd clasped his hands together near the trunk of a pine tree. "I'll boost you up so you can get a better look."

I climbed a few branches and scanned all around.

"Do you see our lodge?" Todd asked.

"Not yet." I edged higher and continued to search.

Todd kept after me. "Anything?"

"Oh no!" I said.

"What? What?" Todd clamored.

My stomach tightened with fear. "You won't believe it."

Todd jumped at the branch, trying to climb up. "What? What?"

"The haunted camp! It's just down the hill," I told him.

"Way to go, Sis," Todd said. "Some leader you are."

"We must have got turned around," I said.

"What's it look like?" Todd asked. "Do you see anyone?"

I shook my head. "All I can see is the lamp in the center of the camp, high on the post."

"What about the rest of the camp?" Todd wondered aloud.

"There are too many trees in the way," I told him. "I can't even see the cabins."

"Then climb higher," Todd urged.

I looked above me. *Why hadn't I picked a bigger tree to climb? These branches looked like sticks. A squirrel could snap them.* "Maybe *higher* is not such a good idea."

Todd wouldn't let up. "Don't be such a chicken."

That did it. I had to go. I grabbed the branch above me and climbed up. It wasn't much thicker than a broom handle. Good thing I didn't weigh much. I kept climbing, higher and higher.

"I can see it," I announced. The cabins looked the same as last night, decaying and burned out. Weeds grew between the stepping stones that went from one building to the next.

"Any sign of the phantom?" Todd asked.

"Not yet." I remembered the phantom's bony, white face and black cape. "And hopefully, there won't be."

Suddenly we heard a wolf howl. *"Ow-woo . . ."*

"Oh, great," I muttered.

Todd shimmied up the trunk, clinging to the bark. The tree began to shake.

"Knock it off," I said.

"Forget you," Todd said. "Wolves can't climb trees. I'm coming up."

I hugged the tree. "Todd, you're making it sway up here."

Another howl, *"Ow-woo . . ."* This time closer.

I looked around, expecting to see the hungry yellow eyes. "Hand me my flashlight," I yelled to Todd.

He tossed it up, but I missed it. "Oh no." It dropped to the ground with a thud. "Todd, get that."

"No way." He clung to the trunk like a monkey.

The tree swayed back and forth. I heard a cracking sound.

"Stop shaking the tree!" I commanded. The ground was twenty feet below me and mostly rocks. *That's going to feel nice,* I thought. I started to climb down, but that was more scary than coming up.

Crack!

I had to do something, quick!

Snap!

Too late. The branch under me came loose and I started to fall.

CHAPTER 12

My feet dangled in the air. I gripped the trunk.
"Are you crazy?" I asked, glaring at my little brother.

"It's not my fault," Todd said. "If I didn't come up, I would have been wolf chow."

Get real, I thought. "That wolf didn't even come close to you."

"That's because I'm up here," he said, embracing the tree like a life preserver.

I scraped my feet along the bark and edged down to a thicker branch. Thank God for protecting us. Talk about a miracle. I looked at the ground far below. I couldn't believe I hadn't fallen. I kept working my way to lower branches. My hands were shaking. I swallowed and tried to catch my breath.

Then I smelled something in the breeze. "What's that?"

Todd balanced on the branch below me. "It smells like smoke."

The burned out cabins came to mind. *Is another one on fire?*

I couldn't see the camp buildings anymore; I was too low in the tree. But I kept my eyes on the bright lamp in the center of the camp.

The smell of smoke grew stronger.

"I see something!" I shouted.

"What?" Todd asked, now sitting on a lower branch.

A thin film of smoke drifted in front of the lamp.

"The camp's on fire again," I yelled. "We've got to put it out."

Todd stayed put. "What about what Mom and Dad said—and the wolf?"

"This is an emergency. And you haven't even seen the wolf," I assured him. "Now get down. Hurry!"

Todd hung from the lowest branch and dropped. I followed. On the ground, I retrieved my light to guide us through the dark trees. We had to move.

"Faster! Keep running," I shouted.

The wolf howled again. *"Ow-woo . . ."*

Footsteps thundered through the woods nearby.

"It's after us," Todd wailed.

Crunch. Snap. Crunch.

"Keep going," I told him.

At the edge of the camp, we saw the flames. The bottom corner of the chapel burned in the night.

We kept running. It wasn't too late. We could put out the fire.

We ran under the lamppost and headed to the right. Almost there.

The howls faded behind us.

Then we saw him. The phantom darted into the open!

He let out a cruel laugh, then disappeared into the forest.

I wanted to run away but couldn't abandon the camp. I remembered what it used to stand for. We had to help.

We found a faucet but it didn't have a hose.

Todd searched the buildings all around. He came back with an old sleeping bag. "We can soak this and smother the flames."

We turned on the faucet and drenched the sleeping bag until we could barely pick it up because of all the water. Together, we held the ends and slapped it against the corner of the chapel. The fire burned like a furnace, undaunted. We could feel the flames on our face.

"It's not working," I shouted.

We dropped the bag and stepped back in horror. The flames climbed higher, lifting into the night. We had to do something. But what?

"We need more water!" Todd shouted.

Running from the flames, we checked the mess hall. Maybe the kitchen would have a bucket. The flashlight led the way, but when we got to the door it was locked. We ran around back, desperate to find something. Then we saw it. A trash can. Perfect!

Taking the can to the faucet, we filled it halfway so that it wasn't too heavy to lift. We each grabbed a side and ran to the flames.

"Ready?" I asked.

Todd gave me the nod.

"Here we go," I shouted. We swung it back and forth. "One, two, three!"

We jerked the trash can forward. The water splashed against the chapel. The fire sizzled.

"It's working!" Todd hollered.

I pulled him toward the faucet. "Quick, let's fill it again."

We repeated the process. This time the flames died down until they were almost out.

Todd patted me on the back. "One more ought to do it."

The third bucket drenched the corner and finished the fire.

Smoke drifted up but nothing more.

Todd gave me a high five. "Way to go partner."

I stepped back, feeling good. We had saved the chapel from destruction. Just then, a red light flashed behind us. We turned to see a police car skidding up. The sheriff jumped out and came right at us. He wore a round hat with a broad bill and a tight, green shirt. He looked as tall as a grizzly bear, and not much happier.

"What's going on here?" he demanded.

I pointed at the chapel. "We just put out a fire."

The sheriff looked at the trash can and mud beneath the blackened corner. "Who started it?"

I shrugged.

Todd spoke up. "I bet it was the phantom."

"The who?" The sheriff looked us over, suspicious.

I started to explain but the sheriff cut me off.

"Turn around and put your hands behind your backs please," he ordered.

We did.

The sheriff patted us down. He found matches in Todd's pocket. My mouth dropped open in shock.

"Todd?" I asked. "Where did those come from?"

"That's what I'd like to know," the sheriff said.

"I always take waterproof matches on hikes," Todd explained. "Just in case we are stranded and need to light a fire."

"You're sure that's the only reason?" the sheriff said.

"Yeah. We came here to help." I looked over my shoulder so I could see the sheriff's face. "You believe us, don't you?"

He stared back, his eyes hard. A steel clicking sound gave us his answer. The sheriff snapped handcuffs on our wrists.

"What's going on?" I asked.

He jerked us toward the patrol car. "You're under arrest for the destruction of private property."

As he led us away we heard the wolf howl. "*Ow-woo . . . !*"

I looked beyond the cabins and saw the hungry, yellow eyes glowing in the night. Then I noticed something else. The wolf wasn't alone!

The phantom stood next to him. With his skeleton face. Smiling.

CHAPTER 13

L ook! He's back there," I pleaded and gestured with my head.

But when the sheriff finally turned to look, the phantom and wolf were gone. After putting us in the car, the sheriff drove us straight to the Mountain Creek police station. There he filled out some paperwork and led us down a dark hallway to a cell.

I grabbed the iron bars and explained what had really happened, for the *umpteenth* time.

"Tell it to the judge," the sheriff told me. "He comes in tomorrow."

Todd sat on the bunk, looking at the stone walls. He tried to figure out what someone had carved into the rock. "Do these lines stand for days?"

"Years," the sheriff said. "And unless I get a hold of your parents, you may be here just as long." He grinned cruelly.

I knew the lodge had a phone, but I didn't know the number. "Can't you just drive us over there?" I asked him, after explaining the directions.

"No can do," he said, turning off the light. He slammed the door at the end of the hall and returned to the front desk area.

We were left alone in the damp, dark cell. *Now what?* I thought. Then it hit me. We could pray. I grabbed Todd's hand and started, "Lord, please help them to find Mom and Dad. And get us out of here."

Todd looked scared. I gave him a hug. His face was sooty from putting out the fire. His hair smelled like smoke. Todd could be a real pest sometimes, but in an emergency he could be really brave. I told him so.

"Thanks, Sis," he said.

We curled up on the cots. Todd closed his eyes. I would have too, but the jail was so creepy. For the next hour I lay there in the dark, keeping watch.

I felt something on my leg.

"What's that?" I squealed, sitting up.

Two huge cockroaches clung to my skin.

"Ahhh! Get off! Get off!" I slapped them away. I

jumped around the cell, screaming! The floor looked like it was moving. Dozens of roaches scurried toward the corners.

"Sick! Gross!" I shrieked.

The outer door unlatched and swung open. The sheriff came rushing down the hall.

"What's going on in here?" he demanded.

Before I could answer, I noticed someone following behind him. I couldn't tell who it was. Then the light came on. I dropped my mouth in shock!

"Dad!" I yelled, holding out my arms.

"Heather! Todd!" Dad exclaimed.

The sheriff unlocked our cell.

Dad rushed inside and Mom followed. They picked us up and held us tight. We shared big family hugs. Then Dad turned to the sheriff. I expected a major argument. No doubt the sheriff would get an earful for locking us up.

But he didn't.

Dad extended a hand. "Thanks, Sheriff. We're grateful for your help."

"Grateful?" I said, irritated. "He locked us up."

The sheriff winked. "That was for your protection. Would you rather have stayed at the camp?"

I thought of those yellow eyes and the phantom's skeleton face. "I guess not," I admitted.

Mom and Dad led us from the cell to the front desk.

"But why did he handcuff us?" I rubbed my wrists.

"We had a long talk with the sheriff," Mom said. "Everything's fine now."

"You're free to go," the sheriff told us. "In fact, on behalf of the department, thanks for putting out the fire." He extended his hand.

Todd shook his hand. "No problem, sir. Anytime. In fact, if you need my help on any other crimes, just give me a jingle."

Dad spoke to the sheriff. "Any idea who started the fire?"

He shook his head. "Nothing solid."

"That's too bad," Mom said.

After a round of good-byes, we piled in the minivan and headed for the lodge. While Dad drove, Mom turned to talk to us. We gave her the whole story.

"I thought we told you to stay away from the camp," she said.

"We tried to," Todd said. "We started out in the opposite direction. But somehow we ended up there."

"Now that's mysterious," Dad admitted.

After cleaning up, I climbed into bed exhausted.

But once again, I couldn't sleep. Turning toward the window, I looked out into the black night. My nose practically touched the glass. The dry branches on the trees looked as creepy as ever, like fingers reaching for me.

"Why can't this glass be thicker?" I muttered. "Bulletproof, even."

It was so thin I could hear everything: the owl hooting, the leaves rustling, the wolf . . .

Oh no! Not again! I sat up.

"*Ow-woo* . . ." The wolf howled. "*Ow-woo* . . ."

I peered through the window.

Was it out there? Could it see me?

"Todd?" I whispered.

He responded with a snore, already sound asleep.

Another howl. "*Ow-woo* . . ."

I squinted again. *There!* In the trees below my window glowed the yellow eyes. The teeth dripped in the night. The wolf howled again and stared right at me!

CHAPTER 14

T odd! Todd!" I wailed.

"*Ow-woo . . .*" the wolf bellowed. It took a step closer to the lodge, staring up at me.

I jumped to Todd's bed and shook him. "Wake up!"

"Leave me alone," he muttered, pulling the covers over his head.

"Todd!" I shouted, bouncing on the bed. I yanked the covers off of him.

He rubbed his eyes. "What?"

"The wolf's here!" I stammered. "Right outside our window!"

Todd sat up and rolled his eyes. "Where?"

"Take a look," I insisted.

He stepped over to my bed and pressed his face against the glass. The window fogged from his breath. "I don't see anything."

I wiped the glass. "His yellow eyes are right there!" I pointed to where the wolf had been, but it was gone.

"Sure it is." Todd gave me a look, then glanced out the window again.

I couldn't believe it. I knew what I'd heard . . . *and seen.*

Todd climbed back in bed. "Heather, if it shows up again, call the dog catcher. I'm sleepy."

I studied the ground outside the window. *Where did it go?* Thank God that Dad had already locked the doors. As long as the wolf stayed *outside,* I could sleep. Lying down again, I closed my eyes. Two seconds later they flicked open again. Who was I kidding? Going to sleep was a joke.

I stared at the ceiling wondering where the wolf had gone. And why it had come. The last time I had seen the wolf, the phantom was nearby. Was *he* out there too? I studied the trees. Stars twinkled between the branches.

"Ow-woo . . ." Another howl.

Now what? Should I wake Todd, or not? Scanning the area beneath my window, I tried in vain to find the wolf. Something moved. But this time it wasn't on the ground.

Like a dark sail in the sky, a shape fluttered through the branches, blocking out the stars as it approached. It stopped, suspended in air, just outside my window.

I choked in horror. The black cape. The skeleton face. The phantom had found us. Hovering like a black bat, he looked right at me and let out a vicious laugh.

At first I almost fainted. Then I heard someone screaming.

It was me. "Ahhh!"

Todd jumped up. "What? What?"

"The phantom!" I stammered, pulling Todd over.

In the dark night the phantom stared right at us. His black cape fluttered in the wind.

"What's he going to do?" Todd whimpered.

The phantom lifted a finger and pointed in our direction.

"What does that mean?" I pleaded.

Swooping forward, he flew right at the window—at us! *He's going to smash through the glass to get us!*

We covered our heads with the blanket and prayed as fast as we could. We expected to hear glass smashing and the sound of cruel laughter. Trembling under the covers, we waited.

And waited.

Nothing happened. We kept waiting. Finally, I couldn't take it anymore. I needed air. Throwing off the covers, we expected to see the phantom's face in the window. He wasn't there. He was gone.

"Where'd he go?" Todd asked.

"Beats me," I said.

Then we heard the creaking of steps inside the house.

Todd swallowed hard. "I think we just found out."

Is that the phantom? I wondered. *Did Dad forget to lock the doors?*

The footsteps grew closer.

Thump. Thump.

He was coming upstairs. To our room. Todd looked at me in horror. There was no time to hide.

The door swung open just as I started to scream.

CHAPTER 15

D ad rushed into the room. "What's wrong? What's wrong?"

"I'm so glad it's you," I said, giving my dad a hug. Then I turned toward the window. "It's out there!"

"What's out there?" he asked.

"The phantom," Todd answered. "The one with the skeleton face."

"And the wolf," I added, still shaking.

Dad looked out the window. Nothing moved. He glanced at us, then back outside. A dead silence filled the night. Even the wind had stopped blowing.

Here we go again, I thought. *Dad won't believe us.* He turned around and sat us down on my bed. I was ready for his "you were only imagining it" speech. But this time I could see the fear in his eyes. There was sweat on his forehead, as if he dreaded what he had to say.

"Something's not right about this," he stated. "I'm going outside to have a look."

"Alone?" I protested. "Can't we go with—"

"You two stay in bed," Dad warned, before letting out a sigh. "I'll check on you when I get back."

He kissed us both then headed downstairs. When the front door slammed shut we pressed our faces to the window to watch. Soon, Dad appeared. He stomped through the woods, searching. His flashlight shined through the trees outside our window. Stopping suddenly, the beam focused on one branch, as if he had found something. Abruptly, he darted out of view.

"There he goes," I said to Todd.

Dad disappeared around the side of the house. As he did, the wolf howled, but in the opposite direction of where Dad had gone. The phantom's laugh came from near the wolf.

"Dad is searching in the wrong place," I told Todd. "He needs to go the other way, toward the camp."

"Maybe he's avoiding my tree snare," Todd suggested.

"You and your traps," I grumbled. "I have to tell Dad where to find the wolf and phantom."

"I'm coming too," Todd announced.

We threw on our clothes.

"*Ow-woo . . .*" The wolf howled.

We ran down the stairs and out the front door.

"Dad?" I shouted. The night air was cold against our skin.

Todd joined in. "Dad!"

We ran around the front of the house, shouting for Dad. *What happened to him?* I wondered. *Was he in danger?* We went to the spot below my window near where the wolf had stood. Huge paw tracks marked the soil.

"Dad!" I called out.

Then another howl echoed off the side of the lodge. I looked at Todd in panic. I shined all around with my flashlight, but Dad was nowhere to be found.

I was about to run back to the lodge when a terrified voice called my name.

"Heather!" Mom shouted, poking her head out of the window. "What are you doing out there?"

"Looking for Dad," I said.

Todd came up beside me. "He's gone."

"He must have come back in," Mom assured us.

"Are you sure?" Todd asked.

Mom looked perplexed. "I heard *someone* come inside."

I thought of the phantom! *Had he lured Dad away, so he could come back for us?* "Stay there,

Mom!" I shouted. "Come on, Todd."

We ran for the front door.

"Wait up, Heather," Todd called, quickly falling behind.

I couldn't wait. Mom needed me.

"Hurry up, Todd," I yelled over my shoulder.

I sprinted ahead, crossing the front porch in two steps. I pushed open the front door.

"Dad! Mom!" I called.

No one answered. I ran through the living room and down the hall.

I cried out again. "You guys! Where are you?"

Still no response. I kept running to the door in front of me. It was my parents' bedroom. I shoved it open, but all I found was an empty room. Mom was gone.

"Mom! Dad!" I started to shake. My heart pounded in my chest. I hunted everywhere: the bathroom, the closet, the kitchen, back down the hall.

Thump. Thump. The sound of footsteps above me.

I ran to the stairs. I could see the faint outline of the moose keeping watch over the den.

Thump. Thump.

Taking the steps two at a time, I reached the top and grabbed for the light switch. Someone's hand was already there.

CHAPTER 16

H eather?" Mom said. She looked panicked.

"Mom, what are you doing?" I gave her a hug. At least she was OK.

"I'm looking for your father. He's gone," Mom shuddered.

"That's what Todd and I have been trying to tell you." I crossed my arms to keep my hands from shaking.

Mom leaned over the rail and searched downstairs. "Where *is* Todd?"

"He was just behind me," I said.

"Where?" Mom demanded, dabbing her nose with a tissue. "I don't see him."

I pointed at the window. "Outside. I ran ahead of him when I came to get you."

"First your father. Now Todd." She ran down the steps and out the front door.

I stayed right behind her. "Todd!" I screamed.

We stopped to listen for him, but he didn't answer. I scanned the dark trees with my flashlight, hoping he would step into view.

Mom jogged around back, still calling his name. She pulled back her hair to listen.

We waited for an answer.

"What was that?" I asked.

Twigs crunched in the woods ahead, toward the camp. We heard a voice.

"Over here!" Todd cried, faintly.

"This way," I said, shining my flashlight on the ground.

We hunched down to get through the branches. The dry bark scraped my skin, but it didn't matter. We had to reach Todd.

"This way," he said.

We chased his voice, using my flashlight to navigate through the trees. It didn't sound like he was far away, and it seemed weird that he wasn't coming to meet us. Then I saw him and knew why.

He was sitting down, with one foot knee-deep in the ground. His own pit snare had gotten the better of him.

"What happened to you?" Mom asked.

"When Heather went inside to find you, I heard something over here. I thought it might be Dad, so

I came to look." Todd bent over to untie the rope cinched around his ankle. "Instead of finding Dad, I found my pit snare instead. Is this thing awesome or what?"

"You have my vote," I said. "You may not be a wild animal, but you definitely belong in a zoo."

"Oh yeah?" Todd challenged. He stood up to get me, but sat back down in a hurry, his face contorted with pain.

"What's wrong?" Mom asked, kneeling beside him.

"I think I twisted my ankle when I landed in here," Todd explained.

After helping him untie the snare, Mom put her arm around Todd's back to help him walk.

I lit the way with my flashlight, more thankful than ever to have new batteries installed. It looked like it was going to be a *long* night.

"Should we call the sheriff?" I asked, as we neared the house.

Mom ignored me and kept walking. When I repeated the question, a strange expression came over her face. But she still didn't answer.

I tried to figure out what was going on. "Mom?"

She stared at me and Todd, like she knew something important but couldn't reveal it.

"What is it?" I asked. "What?"

Mom stopped walking. "Your father already called the sheriff."

"When did he do that?" I asked. "What's going on?"

"Heather, Todd, there's something—" Mom cut herself off. Her mouth dropped open. She gazed over our heads like she was seeing a nightmare. She stepped past us like we didn't exist.

I spun around, expecting to see the wolf or the phantom, but all I saw was an orange light in the distance. Toward the camp.

Fire had returned to the Christian camp. And this time it was raging.

CHAPTER 17

Mom let go of Todd and ran for the lodge. "I've got to call the fire department."

"What were you going to tell us?" I shouted after her.

"Your dad's there," she yelled back.

"Where?" I asked.

She screamed over her shoulder. "AT THE CAMP!"

My eyes met Todd's. Now I understood. Dad had believed our story all along. He must have gone there to catch the phantom. That's why he had called the police.

Todd looked worried. "What if Dad didn't get through to the sheriff? What if Dad's in trouble?"

I didn't want to think about it. But it made sense. Would the camp be on fire if Dad had already caught the phantom? No way. I looked back at the orange glow flickering through the trees. Soon the smell of smoke filled the night. I knew what I had to do. I put my arm around Todd's back and helped him to the porch.

"Tell Mom I went to help Dad," I explained.

Gripping my flashlight, I started running toward the camp. I dodged boulders and jumped over roots. When I came upon the tree snare, I kept wide to the right. The branch still resembled a catapult, bent to the limit. The loop beneath the branch reminded me of an open mouth, hungry for the first foot to come along.

I kept running. As I neared the camp, the trail widened making it easy to pick up speed. *So what if the wolf showed up?* I decided. *If he wants me, he'll have to catch me first.* My arms whipped back and forth. My feet flung ahead. I took longer strides, kicking into a full sprint. *Move it,* I urged myself.

I felt the night air against my face, like my skin was a windshield. Then a movement overhead caught my attention. Something black swooped through the trees. Was the phantom back?

I kept running. All I could think about was reaching the camp. And Dad. The wings screeched and dropped closer. It blended into the darkness. I jumped a log and continued on. A sideache cramped through me like a knife. But I couldn't slow down. *Keep going,* I told myself.

"Screech!" It sounded out.

The wings returned. A huge bat dive-bombed my head! I ducked just in time. Then another bat attacked. And another. I swung the flashlight like a sword, but the bats kept coming.

I tried to dodge them by weaving. But it was no use. I stopped and cowered under a tree for protection, unable to keep going. "What's going on?" I grumbled.

I felt something bite my leg, some kind of bug. I slapped it and lifted my hand. It was a giant mosquito. *Wait a minute,* I thought. *Mosquitoes?*

I used my flashlight to search the area. Mosquitoes were everywhere! And horseflies too! I had stumbled into an insect buffet. That explained it. The bats were starving for something to eat. Either bugs . . . or me! I had to get out of the insect lair.

More bats swooped down. *"Screech!"*

I hunched low to the ground and took off. Slow at first then faster. Running. Sprinting. The wind rushed past as I flew.

The mosquitoes disappeared. The bats faded with them.

They couldn't keep up. I laughed out loud and thanked God for making me so quick and light.

I can run faster than bats can fly, I told myself. *Nothing can catch me!*

My feet glided with ease. No more sideache. My hands cut through the air like rockets.

Crunch! Crunch!

Now what? I cringed.

Crunch! Crunch!

The heavy steps sounded familiar. The wolf was on the hunt. No wonder the bats took off.

"Ow-woo . . . ," the vicious beast howled, not far behind.

I could hear him panting and he was getting closer. I tried to pick up the pace, but the thin mountain air made it hard to breathe. I gripped my flashlight like a club, ready for another fight.

The camp came into view. Only thirty more yards. Just a short dash.

"Ow-woo . . ." the wolf let out.

I beat my hands in the air. My feet kicked ahead, reaching as far as they would go.

The wolf growled. Pine needles snapped under its paws. The distance between us narrowed.

Twenty more yards. I could see the fire. Only a shed near the giant lamp was burning. The rest of the buildings were fine.

But where was Dad?

Crunch! Snap! Grrr!!!

I looked over my shoulder. The wolf was right behind me. The yellow eyes. The razor-sharp teeth. It howled savagely.

Only ten yards to the lamppost.

Could I make it?

Just three strides. Two. One.

I lunged at the pole!

But so did the wolf!

CHAPTER 18

I shinnied up, hugging the post. Higher and higher! The wolf leaped in the air, its teeth dripping. I lifted my feet just a little higher. It barely missed me. The wolf was huge, the size of a lion.

The sweat on my hands caused me to slip. But I kept climbing, squirming farther up the wood pole. Splinters stuck into my hands. My face burned with pain and adrenaline.

The wolf jumped again. I tucked my feet under me, increasing the space between us. It made a third attack. But this time its paws barely left the ground.

"Ow-woo . . ." the wolf howled. It gnawed at the pole in a rage. Barking. Growling.

My lips quivered as I squeezed my arms around the post. How long could I hold on?

"Get out of here!" I shouted, clutching my flashlight.

"Grrr . . ." the wolf growled.

My flashlight! Of course! I aimed the beam at the wolf's eyes. It turned away and barked. The wolf hated the light. It blinded him. No matter where the wolf turned, I shined the flashlight in its eyes.

"Too bad for you, fur ball," I shouted, sensing that the advantage was about to shift in my direction.

The wolf started to back away. It made wider circles around the pole, growling and snapping at me as he went.

This is my chance, I thought. I inched down the pole with the light still blinding the wolf. As long as he couldn't see me, I could run for one of the cabins.

"Lower. Keep the beam on target," I coached myself. "That's it. Lower. Easy. Just a few more feet."

Oops! I lost my grip. The light bobbed and flashed in the sky. The wolf spotted me again. He charged the pole, bounding full speed.

I shimmied higher. *"Quick. Move it!"* I told myself.

The wolf exposed his teeth and growled. I picked up my feet, but I wasn't high enough. I had to do something. But what? I couldn't rely on my flashlight this time. Or could I?

The wolf sprang through the air, flying straight at me. I hurled my flashlight in defense.

Whack! The wolf let out a yelp as the heavy flashlight knocked him on the head.

I climbed higher.

The wolf scratched the flashlight in the dirt. He looked up at me and growled. His yellow eyes burned. Once again I was safe. The wolf couldn't jump this high.

All at once, the shed caught my attention. It burned like crumpled papers, bright and hot. The flames climbed higher, filling the night. Wood creaked and splintered. Embers popped. The frame swayed and started to fall. I turned my face from the heat as the fire crackled and devoured the wood.

With a final sigh, the shed collapsed. Flames shot everywhere. Embers spiraled through the sky like a volcanic eruption. I had to close my eyes.

"Yelp! Yelp!" the wolf barked in pain. A burning board torched his tail.

It yelped again and took off.

"Serves you right," I yelled, watching the wolf disappear in the woods. So much for Fido the fur ball.

Then I remembered Dad and feared the worst. Was he trapped in the shed before it caught on fire? Was he in there? Under the flames?

"Dad," I shouted. "Dad!"

I scrambled down the post and studied the rubble and embers. It was too hot to get close. I had to block my face with my hand and peer through my fingers.

"Dad! Dad!" I screamed, scared to death. "Dad!"

I ran around the collapsed shed, shielding my face from the heat. The flames warmed the dark sky.

"Dad, answer me!" I wailed. I studied the fire, praying he wasn't in there.

"Heather! Heath—" a voice called. But then it cut off.

I spun around and shouted again. "Dad?"

No answer. But that was his voice. I knew it. He was OK. And somewhere in the camp.

But where? And why didn't he respond?

The fire popped and crackled. Embers glowed with heat.

I ran to the pole to get my flashlight. I had to find Dad and help him.

"*Ow-woo . . .*" The wolf let out a howl and circled nearby. He wouldn't charge the flames, but he watched me, waiting for his chance.

If only I could stay here, warm and safe by the fire. But I couldn't. I had to leave the burned down shed to search for my dad. It sounded like his voice came from the cabin area, up the slope to the left of the lamppost. I didn't know which cabin, but I'd start with the nearest one. With a good start I could make it.

The wolf growled, keeping its distance.

"God speed my feet," I whispered in prayer. I crouched down like a sprinter.

No more shouting, I decided. *If the phantom has captured Dad, I need to sneak up on them.* I took a last look over my shoulder. No wolf in sight.

Ready. Set. Go! My feet launched ahead. My arms pumped back and forth. I kept low to the ground, running toward the cabins and Dad's voice.

Crunch! Snap! The wolf charged with fury and rage. *Grrrr!* The pursuit was on.

Here we go again, I thought.

The beast closed in, ready to devour me. I bolted like lightning to the porch. With my arm extended like a battering ram, I slammed through the unlocked door.

The wolf charged full speed. I turned around and gasped! He was just yards away. Feet. Inches. Grabbing the door, I slammed it shut. The latch clicked just as the wolf bashed face first into the other side.

Grrrr. It scratched at the wood. It gnawed the doorknob with its teeth. I remembered the story of a dog that chewed through a door to save its owner from a fire. If a dog could do that, so could a wolf. But it wouldn't be to save me.

Scratch! Scratch! The wolf gnawed at the outside. Pieces of rotted wood fell from beneath the doorknob. I felt like the second little pig in that children's story. How long would the cabin last? I had to do something.

Taking hold of a bunk bed, I slid it in front of the door. Whew! Safe at last. You snooze you lose, Mr. Big Bad Wolf. I sat down on the bed to catch my breath. Then something occurred to me.

"Dad?" I asked softly, hoping and praying. I realized that he might be in the cabin with me.

No one answered.

I had dropped my flashlight on the bunk when I moved it. I reached for the light, eager to have a look around. My hand squeezed something with claws and fur.

"Yuck!" I squealed, letting go.

The animal hissed and crawled across my lap.

"Ahhh!" I screamed. Standing up, I flung the thing across the room. It landed with a thud and hissed all the louder. Once again I grabbed for my flashlight, this time more frantically than ever. But all I could feel was the mattress. Where was my flashlight? My fingers scrambled all around.

There! I found it. I shined the light in the direction of the sound.

Two beady eyes stared back at me. Ready to attack!

CHAPTER 19

A massive rat hissed with rage! Its lips were peeled back, exposing its teeth. For a moment I though it was an opossum. The rat darted at the light, then to the side. Soon more rats appeared and scurried toward me. Their claws scraped the wood floor.

What next? I thought. *A dozen raptors with revolvers?*

I picked up my feet and pulled my knees to my chin. The rats stalked me, hissing and showing their teeth. I edged to the back of the mattress until my back pressed against the door. The wolf growled on the other side and scratched at the wood.

The rats climbed each end of the bunk bed. They had me surrounded. I had to get out, but the door was blocked and the wolf was waiting.

Hiss! The rats came closer.

I searched the cabin with my flashlight. There had to be a way out.

Suddenly a black rat crossed the mattress, charging me. I grabbed my flashlight like an aluminum bat. I'd always liked softball. Time to play rat ball.

Smack!

"Rat in right field," I called out.

It landed across the room with a thud.

The commotion intensified. Another rat came at me.

Whack!

"Down the line for a double," I said triumphantly.

My smile faded as more rats climbed the mattress. Far more than I could hit.

Hiss! Hiss! They scratched with their claws and exposed their teeth. A few climbed the bunk overhead, ready to pounce from above.

I had to escape and soon! I searched the room. The light beam scanned the bare walls.

There! On the opposite side of the cabin I spied an open window above the top bunk. I could squeeze through to the outside. I checked the distance across the room. A few good jumps and I could make it.

"Hold still," I told myself, wanting the rats to come to this side of the room. That didn't take long. They scurried along the floor and rafters, converging.

I squatted on the mattress. My arms wrapped around my shins. I was ready to triple jump across the floor and high jump to the upper bunk.

Hiss, hiss, scratch, hiss. The rats smelled blood, or at least *thought* they did.

Closer. Closer.

Now!

I sprang from the mattress! One step. Two. Three. I crossed the room. The rat army turned and charged after me. Hissing. Scratching. Eyes gleaming.

I grabbed the bed frame and climbed to the top bunk. I made it!

The wolf remained on the other side of the building, growling and gnawing at the door. I had to be quiet. The next cabin seemed a mile away, but maybe Dad was there. I would have to outrun the wolf to find out.

I poked my head out the window. It was a short drop. I turned around to put my feet out first. The rats closed in. *Hiss!* I wouldn't miss *that* sound. One darted across the bunk toward my face.

Whack! Home run.

I shoved my legs out of the window. They dangled in the air. "Here goes nothing," I decided. I let go. When my feet hit the ground I rolled.

Rising up, I started for the next cabin. Then I heard a voice and stopped. It sounded like Dad's. But the voice came from across the camp near the mess hall. I started down the slope, sprinting as fast as I could.

"Grrr . . . ."

"Not again!" I cried, glancing over my shoulder.

The wolf rounded the cabin in hot pursuit. I kept going. The wolf bounded ahead, snapping at my heels. Just a few more feet and I'd be in the mess hall. Then a thought occurred to me. *What if the door was locked like yesterday?* I'd be a goner. But what else could I do? I didn't have a choice. Running on, I reached the door. I grabbed the doorknob and turned. It opened!

Inside, I slammed the door and kept going. I hoped the doorknob would hold. Just in case it didn't, I put some distance between me and the wolf. I made my way across the dining area to the kitchen. Then I turned to look, wondering *what now?* The wolf scratched and clawed. It slammed against the door, again and again.

Then silence. What happened? Had he left?

Yeah right. In my dreams.

The wolf's shadow appeared in the air like a stealth fighter. *Crash!* It smashed through the window next to the door. Glass burst into the dining hall as the wolf landed. He shook his wiry fur from head to toe, like he was wringing out after a bath. Bits of glass flew in every direction. I didn't know if I should run for my life or stop to shake his paw. He was amazing!

My admiration quickly disappeared when the wolf caught sight of me and howled. Ducking into the kitchen, I was more determined than ever to get away. Searching over the counters and appliances, I wondered where I could hide. I looked for anything. "Please, Lord," I begged. "I know you're with me . . . and I need help!"

Then I saw it—a walk-in freezer with a huge, stainless steel door. I remembered what Todd had taught me about trapping wild animals. Lure them into the cage, then close the door. That's it! Todd, you're a genius.

I went inside and climbed the highest rack, right by the door. The latch looked like it could take anything. I waited, praying my trick would work. Soon, I could hear the wolf approaching, panting, growling. His claws clicked on the tile floor.

Almost here. Any second.

The wolf ran in! Right below me! Now!

I jumped out and slammed the door shut. The heavy latch came down hard. The wolf jerked around and growled inside, but the door was so thick I could barely hear him.

"Take it easy, Fido," I laughed over my shoulder. "You're not going anywhere."

I walked across the kitchen and into the dining hall, thinking I could finally catch my breath.

Wrong again.

All at once I heard the stainless steel door swing open and the wolf growling for blood. *There's no way he could have opened that door,* I fumed. *The phantom must have freed him.* I ran back outside, desperate for a new plan. The first thing I noticed was the chain-link fence that surrounded the pool. Finally, something that the wolf couldn't get through. After climbing over the fence, I paused to see what would happen. That's when I noticed Todd on the far edge of the camp, near the trail that led to our lodge.

"Todd, hide!" I screamed.

"What?" he yelled back.

I didn't have time to warn him again. The wolf burst from the mess hall and charged straight for Todd.

"No!" I shouted. I rattled the fence and screamed, hoping the wolf would stop and come toward me. But my trick didn't work. Todd stood frozen, too scared to move as the wolf bounded straight for him.

"Todd, run!" I wailed.

Finally, Todd turned and disappeared down the trail as the wolf bore down. Todd wasn't very fast to begin with, and with his twisted ankle, I feared the worst.

Scaling back over the fence, I moved to the lamppost, not sure what to do. I wanted to help Todd, but how? Hopefully, he would be up a tree before the wolf got near him. Besides, I still had to find Dad. I stood awkwardly under the bright light, frustrated. But not for long. The *swoosh* of a tree branch, followed by loud yelping, settled the issue. Todd had lured the wolf after him on purpose, just to draw it into the tree snare. And it worked. The wolf whimpered and howled into the night, all strung up with nowhere to go.

"Todd, you're the best," I called out.

With the wolf finally out of the way, I returned to the mess hall. Since the phantom hadn't shown his face, I decided to quit worrying about him. He was probably long gone by now.

Halfway across the mess hall I stopped. The kitchen door swung open and the phantom stepped into view just a few feet away.

"Not you!" I whimpered, ready to faint.

A cruel grin spread across his skeleton face as he stared right at me . . . and laughed.

CHAPTER 20

I backed up, taking short nervous breaths. "What do you want?"

The phantom didn't answer. He grabbed at me with his bony white hand. I smacked it away with my flashlight. He lunged forward, burning mad, but I jumped to the side just in time and took off across the dining hall.

The phantom followed.

I couldn't let him catch me. I had to escape and find Dad.

The phantom closed in. His heavy footsteps sounded like thunder behind me.

I weaved through the chairs like a running back, my heart racing. Then a plan came to mind. I'd let the phantom get closer on purpose. I dodged more tables and chairs but at a slower pace.

He closed in. Closer. Closer. The phantom reached for me—.

Now! I grabbed a chair and slid it behind me, right in front of the phantom. He couldn't react in time.

Bam! The phantom tumbled over the chair and smashed into a table, knocking the legs out from under it. Before he could get up, the table collapsed on top of him.

I put distance between us, then chanced a look back. The phantom shoved the table aside and rose to his feet. He stumbled after me. He wasn't laughing now.

If I could make it outside, lots of buildings covered the hillside. I could hide in one. If more rats came, I would smack them away. If the phantom didn't have a flashlight, he might not be so fortunate. We'd see how high he flew with twenty rats hanging on his cape.

I searched for a way of escape. With the phantom between me and the front door, that wasn't an option. I needed another way.

The phantom limped toward me, his face hard. I had to find something. Fast!

Wait a minute. Steps! They climbed the back wall to a second story, but where did they lead? Offices? More classrooms? If I climbed them, could I get back down? Or would I be cornered?

The phantom kept coming. He didn't say a word, but his hands swung with rage as he flung chairs out of the way.

I didn't have a choice. I bounded up the stairs, moving so quickly the Lord must have lifted me. At the top I pushed through a door. I tried to lock it behind me but it wouldn't. Time to hide. I shined my flashlight all around. I was at the end of a long hall with doors lining each side. Lots of doors.

I could hear the phantom hobbling up the stairs. *Step . . . Bump. Step . . . Bump.*

Which door should I choose? I had to decide.

Step . . . Bump. Step . . . Bump.

I tried the first door. It was locked. The second. Also locked. The third. It opened! But the phantom would discover it too.

I ran down to the fifth. Locked. The sixth. *Open.* I went inside and softly closed the door behind me. It wouldn't lock! I took a quick scan with my flashlight. I was in an office.

The door at the top of the stairs slammed open. *Step . . . Bump. Step . . . Bump.* A doorknob rattled. The phantom was trying the doors.

I had to hide. But where? I opened the closet. Empty. Bad idea. Nothing to hide behind. Under the desk? Wrong. An easy search.

What about the window? Was there a fire escape? I pushed open the curtains. No fire escape, but it had a ledge. I pried open the window. It was a twenty-foot drop. The ledge was a foot wide. *I can do this.*

Step . . . Bump. Step . . . Bump. Another door-knob shook.

I crept onto the ledge and closed the window behind me. I pressed my back against the wall. Carefully, I slid my feet along. I felt like a captured sailor walking the plank. *Easy does it. Don't look down,* I reminded myself. I clutched my flashlight for dear life.

Several feet from the window, I stopped. The branches from a nearby tree practically touched my nose. Holding my breath, I listened for the phantom.

Creak. The sound of dry hinges shattered the silence.

Step . . . Bump. Step . . . Bump. The phantom limped closer.

I waited. But nothing happened. I saw a flashlight scanning the office I had just come from. *Some phantom,* I scoffed. *He can't even see in the dark.*

Or could he?

A skeleton face appeared in the window. I flattened myself against the wall, hoping he wouldn't see me. A moment later the phantom stepped back out of view.

I breathed a sigh of relief. Then suddenly the window slid open!

The phantom shoved his head outside and looked right at me with his skeleton face. Extending himself, he grabbed for my arm. I edged away, pressing my back against the building.

The phantom stuck one foot on the ledge and reached for me. I tried to scoot away but couldn't. I was at the end of the ledge. What if he came out? I looked at the branch swaying in the breeze. I could easily reach it. But would it hold me? A rush of confidence filled my heart. They didn't call me Heather the Feather for nothing.

The phantom stepped out on the ledge. He edged closer.

The branch will hold, I told myself. I prayed for strength . . . and good distance. Another few inches and the phantom would have me. I shoved the flashlight into my pocket.

And jumped!

My heart dropped.

But my feet flew. The wind swept under me. I sailed forward like an eagle. My fingers like talons, soaring. I grabbed the branch and held tight. The branch plunged, bending low like Todd's snare. Then it cracked.

"Don't break," I pleaded.

It didn't. The branch began to rise, lifting me higher. It held! I had made it. I climbed to the trunk of the tree.

The phantom watched me in shock—stunned and furious. He examined the distance between the ledge and the tree. Would he come too? The phantom extended his hand—debating.

I worked my way through the branches, lowering myself. No time to waste. I kept an eye on the phantom. Would he go for it? I had to get away and find Dad while I had the chance.

The phantom took another look at the branch. Then he climbed back inside.

It felt good to see him chicken out. "I guess you're not flying so high *now*, are you?" I yelled after him. I thought of him outside my window earlier in the night. If he could swoop through the trees then, why not now?

Hanging from the lowest branch, I dropped to the ground. I ran quickly to check one of the dormitory buildings further up the hill. I heard Dad's voice, but it seemed far away. The farther I went, the longer it would take the phantom to find me.

A muffled cry stopped me in my tracks. It sounded like it came from the chapel, back down the hill. I sprinted down the slope, keeping an eye out for the phantom. Fortunately he still hadn't emerged from the mess hall.

Like the rest of the camp buildings, the chapel was in bad shape. Boards covered a few of the windows. Black soot clung to the corner that was burned by the fire earlier in the night.

Pushing through the door, I stepped quietly into the chapel. I couldn't call out for fear the phantom would hear my voice and come running. I held my breath, listening. But nothing stirred, I feared the worst.

Turning on my flashlight, I was shocked by what I saw.

"I don't believe it!" I gasped.

CHAPTER 21

It was my dad! His wrists and ankles were bound by ropes. A handkerchief covered his mouth. He lifted his head from the pew he was lying on and squinted into the flashlight beam.

"Dad? Are you OK?" I cried. I ran over and threw my arms around him.

He stared at me with a mixture of joy and fear.

I worked to free him as fast as I could. His mouth was first. The knot held its grip like a steel cable. It hurt my fingers to pry it loose. But I pushed and tugged until it finally gave way.

"Heather," Dad whispered. "You shouldn't have come here."

"But Dad," I protested. "I saw the flames and smoke. As soon as I found out you were here, I had to come." The knots behind Dad's back came next.

I jerked and pulled like crazy. They eased some, but not enough.

Dad just kept shaking his head. "I never should have brought you here. It was a mistake. It's just that I had no idea . . ." He paused, as if still in shock over what was happening.

"About what?" I asked. The knots held tight. My hands felt weak, useless.

"That he would go this far," Dad said.

My mouth dropped open. "What do you mean, *he?* You know about the phantom?"

"Sort of," Dad admitted. "My company insures this camp. Over the last few years, several property claims have been filed. The owners argued that someone was trying to destroy them. After hearing their story I decided to check things out myself. I planned to inspect the grounds, interview a few people, then make a report. No big deal. I thought there would still be plenty of time for us to enjoy as a family."

I strained at the ropes. They began to come loose. "But you totally brushed off what we said about the phantom, like there's no such thing."

Dad tipped his head to the side. "There is, and there isn't."

"What do you mean?" I asked.

Before Dad could answer, we heard footsteps

moving across the pine needles in our direction.

"He's on his way," Dad warned. "You've got to hide."

I glanced around. "Where?"

"Up there."

Not far above us, horizontal beams stretched from one side of the chapel to the other. Vertical beams rested on top of the horizontal ones, angling up to the A-frame roof. It looked a lot like an attic would if you could see the woodwork from below.

"What if the phantom sees me?" I questioned, dreading the thought.

"He won't," Dad said with confident faith. "God had lots of reasons for making you the way you are. This is one of them."

Step . . . bump. Step . . . bump. The phantom was close.

I stared at my skinny legs and thin frame. God knew what he was doing. I could lie on the beam and never be seen from the chapel floor.

Dad stood up and steadied himself. With his feet still tied together it wasn't easy, but the ropes were getting looser by the minute.

"Before you climb up," he whispered. "Fix my gag so the phantom won't know you were here."

I quickly retied the bandanna, but not as tight. Standing on the back of a pew, I climbed onto his shoulders. From there I grabbed the beam and pulled myself up. I stretched out flat, arms at my sides, palms down.

"Perfect," Dad mumbled. "You can't be seen." He struggled against the ropes. "And I'm almost free."

Just then, the door burst open. The phantom stomped inside. I heard his heavy boots on the wood floor.

"Where is she?" the phantom demanded in a raspy, low voice.

I realized that I had never heard the phantom speak before. I thought I recognized the voice.

My dad just mumbled, like he couldn't answer because of the gag.

The phantom limped around. He shined his flashlight toward me. The light searched along the length of the rafter. I saw it glide by like a spotlight. I held my breath and kept perfectly still.

The light dropped down. *It worked!* The phantom had given up. That's all Dad needed to see. I heard the sound of ropes dropping to the ground.

"How did you—?" the phantom choked.

Dad jumped up and knocked the phantom to the ground in mid-sentence.

I had to see this. I peeked over the beam. The phantom slammed against the wall. Dad wasn't a happy camper. He scooped up the ropes and moved forward to tie up the phantom.

The phantom twisted away. He lunged at Dad and knocked him down. Now Dad was in trouble!

I had to do something. But what?

Then it hit me. I could drop in, unexpected, with a steel flashlight armed and ready. I'd knock the phantom on the head and let Dad take care of the rest.

But who was I kidding? What if the phantom saw me coming and moved out of the way. I'd be a goner. Still, I had to do something. I couldn't just hide and let the phantom get Dad. I tried to psych myself up. I thought of that verse that says, "Greater is he who is in you, than he who is in the world." That helped. My hands stopped trembling and I gripped my flashlight like a club.

The phantom stepped back and grabbed a chair. He lifted it high in the air to crash it down on Dad's back.

I couldn't wait any longer. It had to be now. *Ready or not, phantom, here I come.*

CHAPTER 22

I rolled off the beam and dropped straight down. Clutching the flashlight with both hands, I knocked the phantom on the head. He stumbled for a few feet, then crumpled to the ground.

Dad got up and grabbed the ropes. The phantom grumbled while holding his head. The deep, raspy voice sounded familiar. He started to rise to his feet.

"Hurry, Dad," I yelled. I held my flashlight tight, ready to help.

No need.

Dad tackled the phantom from behind. The phantom tripped forward and bumped his head on the wall. That did it. He was out cold. Just to be safe, Dad tied the phantom's hands and feet together.

"Dad!" I ran over and gave him a hug. He squeezed me tighter than ever before, like he would never let go. After everything I'd been through, it felt good to be in his arms and safe.

"The sheriff will take it from here," Dad said.

Dad turned the phantom over. I hid my eyes immediately. Just the sight of his creepy face gave me the chills.

"It's OK, Heather," Dad assured me. "It's just a cheap mask." He peeled it off.

"The man from the hardware store!" I exclaimed.

"You got it. Meet Stan Fowles, the owner of Mountain Creek Hardware," Dad announced.

I shook my head, mystified.

Dad explained the story. "Remember when I said there is and there isn't such a thing as a phantom? What I meant was, technically, they don't exist. Sure, phonies will come along to mislead people and scare them away. But there's no such thing as a real phantom with supernatural powers."

"But I saw him flying outside my window," I protested.

"Just a trick," Dad explained. "He was swinging from cables. I found them when I went down to check."

"Why did he want to scare people away?" I asked, still full of questions.

Dad put his arm on my shoulder. "When Fowles bought the hardware store a few years ago, he started selling building supplies to this camp. But the supplies were defective, factory rejects. Fowles bought them at a discount, then sold them to the camp at full price. Before long, things started to break and fall apart. A roof even collapsed."

"Was anyone hurt?" I asked.

"Fortunately, no. No one was in the cabin at the time. They were supposed to be, but the counselor said he just felt led to take his campers on an evening walk. Everyone knew that God had protected them," Dad said.

"That's for sure," I agreed.

Dad continued, "Since my company insured the camp, we paid to fix the roof right away. But when we discovered that the materials were defective, we asked Mr. Fowles to pay the cost of repair."

"What did he do?" I asked.

"He refused to pay," Dad answered. "The camp stopped doing business with him immediately. So did the people in town."

Suddenly the dust in the Mountain Creek Hardware store made sense. That merchandise had sat there for months without being touched.

"Is that why Fowles vowed to destroy the camp?" I asked.

Dad nodded. "He even trapped that wolf and brought it here to scare the campers. Anything for revenge."

"But why was he after us?" I wanted to know.

"He knew that my report would provide enough money to rebuild the camp. He also knew that he would be going to jail," Dad explained.

I pictured the wolf's razor-sharp teeth. "Dad, why didn't you tell us all this sooner?"

His eyes filled with regret. "I wasn't sure until tonight. But when I followed him here, I found out the truth. I'm sorry you had to go through all this."

Crunch! Crunch! Heavy steps approached from outside, crossing the dry pine needles and leaves.

"What's that?" I asked. Was the wolf loose again? Something was approaching fast, and heading straight for us, just a few feet away. It crossed the porch.

The door burst open!

CHAPTER 23

Nobody move!" a gruff voice shouted.

I stood, petrified. Did the phantom have an accomplice?

When I saw who it was, my fear quickly turned to relief. The sheriff stood with his feet firmly planted. He flashed his light on me and Dad, then in the phantom's face. "Looks like I'm a little late," he admitted.

"Better late than never," I said with a smile.

The sheriff dragged the phantom to his feet and slapped on the handcuffs. "Well, Fowles, it looks like you've terrorized this camp for the last time." The sheriff tugged on the phantom's arm and led him outside.

It was then that Dad and I paused to appreciate the chapel. No wonder the old woman in Mountain

Creek raved about its beauty. Polished hardwoods of various shades lined the walls and formed the pews. And thanks to the bright lamp outside, the stained glass windows radiated with color, each with a different scene from the Bible. Of the many windows, the one at the front of the sanctuary was the most spectacular of all. Shades of red, blue, yellow, and purple sparkled like jewels, each drawing the eye to the gold cross in the center.

"What a refreshing sight that is," Dad said, staring at the cross.

"That's for sure," I added.

We stood there for a few minutes then headed outside. Once the phantom was put in the squad car, I told the sheriff where I thought he would find the wolf and Todd.

"The wolf?" the sheriff asked. "Is that thing really back?"

"Back and badder than ever," I said. "Look what he did to the mess hall."

As soon as the sheriff saw the broken glass, he grabbed his gun. "If the wolf did that, you'd better get me to it, and fast."

We started down the slope toward the trailhead, but hardly got past the lamppost when we heard something.

"What was that?" I asked.

"It came from over there," Dad said, pointing toward the trees at the edge of the camp.

Crunch! Crunch! Pine needles snapped under foot.

Something occurred to me. After the phantom had retreated from the ledge, he disappeared for a while before coming to the chapel. What if somehow he freed the wolf? And what if the wolf went after Todd?

I stared at the dark shadows moving in the trees. Would the wolf bolt from the woods to get me, even with Dad and the sheriff here?

Crunch! Crunch! More twigs snapped.

The sheriff raised his gun to defend us.

My heart pounded.

Swoosh! The leaves pushed aside.

I was shocked again. But this time, in a good way. Todd and Mom stepped into the open. Once they saw us, they ran over and we shared a big family hug. Soon two firemen in heavy, yellow coats emerged from the same section of trees.

"What happened to the wolf?" the sheriff asked, putting his gun away.

The firemen just grinned and waited for Todd to respond.

Todd shrugged. "I'm sure the wolf would *like* to be here, but he's all tied up at the moment."

We enjoyed a much needed laugh as Todd described his tree snare to the sheriff. He also explained that Mom had stayed back to help him.

"It's a good thing the trap worked," Mom added. "Or even *I* would have been up a tree."

"Excellent job, young man," the sheriff said, shaking Todd's hand. "I'll give Fish and Game a call and let them take care of it from here."

"Already done," the fireman with the mustache said. "Since the blaze died out before we arrived, we shifted our attention to the wolf—not that Todd needed our help."

"What can I say?" Todd offered. "Beware of the snare."

"What will they do to the wolf now?" I asked.

"I imagine Fish and Game will take him back to the wilderness where he belongs," the sheriff told me. "Far from civilization *and* this Christian camp!"

Hearing the word *Christian* reminded me of why the camp was built in the first place. Looking around at the cabins and buildings, and finally the chapel, I prayed that with the phantom and wolf out of the way, the camp would reopen soon, and kids would come to learn about God just like they used to. I walked to the center of the camp and stood under the lamppost, thankful to have had such a bright light when I needed it most.

Soon, my family joined me, followed by the firemen. But the sheriff just stood in place, his eyes wide. When I waved him over, he didn't respond. He stared up at the lamp in awe.

"Well, I'll be," he finally muttered.

"What is it?" Dad asked.

"I don't believe it," the sheriff confessed. He continued to watch the lamp, mystified.

"What?" we all wondered. "What is it? Tell us."

The sheriff shrugged and filled us in. "There's no electricity in this camp. The power was shut off months ago."

"Now that's a miracle!" Todd gasped.

With broad smiles on our faces, we all stared at the light above us.

Then I noticed a plaque at the base of the post with a verse inscribed in it. Without hesitating, I read it for everyone.

"When Jesus spoke again to the people, he said, 'I am the light of the world. Whoever follows me will never walk in darkness, but will have the light of life.' John 8:12."

"Amen to that," the sheriff agreed, still watching the lamp. "Amen to that."

As we turned to leave, I thanked God for everything he had done, including the way he created each one of us—even me, Heather the Feather—alive and well, in the light of life.

The End

Don't miss another exciting

HEEBIE JEEBIES

adventure!

Turn the page to check out a chapter from

THE RAT THAT ATE POODLES

CHAPTER 7

I had to be sure. I was tired of being so confused. I had to know if this was really happening or if I was going crazy. I had to find out if there really was a giant, mutant rat prowling the neighborhood or whether it was all in my wild imagination. Whichever way it turned out, it wouldn't be much fun—but at least I'd know for sure.

My plan was to stay awake until Truman started barking. Then I'd sneak down into the backyard with my flashlight and baseball bat and see if this was all in my head. I was terrified, but it was something I knew I had to do.

When I went to bed that night, I kept my jeans and tee shirt on and pulled the covers over me. I hung my Chicago Bulls windbreaker over the chair at my desk and put my flashlight in the pocket. I also made sure it had fresh batteries. I propped my aluminum baseball bat next to my dresser. When I heard Mom and Dad coming up to say good night, I pulled the covers up to my chin.

My door opened quietly, and Dad peeked in. When he saw I was awake, he and Mom came in and stood at the side of my bed.

"You're making some real progress in the garage," Dad said. "You've been doing some good, hard work. I'm proud of you, Daniel. Real proud."

"We didn't even have to tell him to go to bed tonight," Mom said to Dad. "He came up here by himself."

Mom bent over and kissed me on the forehead. I held the covers tightly under my chin.

"My son," she said straightening up. "He's so responsible all of a sudden."

When Mom and Dad closed the bedroom door behind them, I rolled over and switched off my bedside lamp. I lay there in the dark looking at my window and thinking about what Mom had said. I had a creepy, sinking feeling. Mom was right. Maybe I *was* responsible—responsible for creating a monster!

Suddenly I realized I'd been sleeping—I had that bad taste in my mouth. I rolled over and looked at the clock. A quarter to three.

I listened for Truman's barking, but I didn't hear him. In fact I didn't remember hearing him at all that night. *What woke me up, then?* I laid my head back on my pillow and yawned. I was warm and sleepy. It was the middle of the night. Suddenly, going out in the backyard to look for a monster didn't seem like such a hot idea. I just wanted to roll over and go back to sleep.

Then I heard it. It sounded like someone sweeping a rough wooden floor with a broom. I held my breath and listened. Soon there was a scratching noise; then a loud klunk and a tearing noise, coming from the backyard. Now I knew what had wakened me.

I went to the window and looked down into the yard. It was cloudy tonight, so there was no moon to light the yard at all. I couldn't even make out the shape of the clubhouse, it was so dark out there.

I rolled out of bed and pulled on my jacket. I checked in the pocket for my flashlight. I slipped on my shoes and tied the laces. My fingers tingled, and it was hard to make a bow. I felt around in the dark until I found my baseball bat. My mouth felt dry. I opened my bedroom door as quietly as I could and crept downstairs.

I tiptoed past the humming refrigerator and the dripping kitchen faucet. I paused with my hand on the cold kitchen doorknob. It took me a minute to gather up the courage to open the door. I twisted the knob and pulled. The door creaked slowly open, and I felt the night air on my face.

I peered into the dark backyard. With the door open, the commotion sounded much louder. There was a thumping noise and a wheezing. I decided to leave the door open, in case I needed to get back inside fast. I swallowed hard and stepped down onto the back steps, shining the flashlight all around in the darkness. My hand was shaking, so the flashlight's beam did too.

I inched toward the open garage as quietly as I could, stepping over an old record player and shuffling around a bag of rusty golf clubs. There was so much junk arranged in the driveway now, it was hard to move without making noise. I held the baseball bat high in my right hand, ready to club anything that rushed at me.

I froze. The noises had stopped. All I could hear was the chirping of crickets in distant yards. The breeze stirred the hairs on the back of my neck. I shone my light through the open garage door. The shaky beam ran along all the junk stacked up high. Shadows crawled along the walls as I slowly moved the beam of light from one side of the garage to the other. It lit up the rafters full of cobwebs and the swirls of dust in the air. I stood still and listened. I held my breath, waiting.

The noises began again—but they weren't in the garage. They were coming from somewhere in the dark backyard. I threaded my way among the boxes and old furniture and stood on the edge of the back garden. I shone the light around Mom's flower beds. Nothing was moving. My right arm was getting tired from holding the bat aloft, so I switched hands, careful not to drop the flashlight. I stepped over Mom's flower bed onto the lawn.

A loud thump made me jump. I stabbed the light toward the clubhouse door where the noise had come from. The beam lit up two red eyes in the dark. A long, pink tail dangled from the doorway. The beam of light began to shake uncontrollably. I wanted to yell, but I couldn't breathe. I stood there frozen in fear.

The two eyes peered at me from the dark doorway. They looked evil and angry in the shaking light. The giant rat didn't move. It held perfectly still and stared at me coldly from the shadows. My legs felt like rubber. I gripped the baseball bat tightly and slowly stepped backward toward Mom's flower bed and the concrete driveway.

I was inching my way back toward the open kitchen door when the thing snorted at me angrily. I dropped my flashlight and bat and dashed toward the door, plowing through Mom's flower bed, tripping over boxes and knocking down furniture as I clambered across the driveway cluttered with junk. I heard things clanking and clattering to the ground behind me. It sounded like the rat was right behind me.

I leaped up the back steps to the open kitchen door without looking back. I had no idea how close behind me the monster was. As I slammed the door and twisted the lock, my heart was pounding crazily. I pressed my weight against the door for a few seconds and then sprinted through the kitchen and up the stairs to my room. I jumped into bed and yanked the covers over my head.

In a few minutes I got my breath back—and a little bit of my courage. I crept to my open bedroom window and peered down into the yard. My flashlight lay on the lawn, lighting up a triangle of grass and making it hard to see anything else in the yard.

After a few seconds, the noises began again—a thumping and wheezing in the clubhouse. I closed the window and latched it tight.

I lay on my bed again and stared at the ceiling, trying to think of what to do now that I was sure.

Mom was right; I *was* responsible. I'd created this monster.

Now how was I going to get rid of it?

More exciting releases from

THE NEW QUICK-READING TALES THAT ENTERTAIN WHILE AFFIRMING THE PRESENCE AND POWER OF GOD!

Daniel Larkin is cleaning out the garage when he spills some mysterious bottles from his dad's old chemistry set. He intends to hide the evidence and keep his mouth shut, but that becomes more difficult when a giant mutant rat grows from out of the chemicals. Daniel is terrified by this giant red-eyed, pink-tailed, dog-eating rodent and plagued by his own guilty conscience in this fun, creepy, and ultimately uplifting story of a kid who learns that covering up a mistake can be the biggest mistake of all.

The Rat That Ate Poodles   0-8054-0170-9